Riley Tune

WARPER: ORIGINS

Table of Contents

ACKNOWLEDGMENTS

I would like to thank the following for their help and support: First and foremost, the LORD, I am thankful for the life I have and the ability to create worlds within my mind to make something beautiful; my parents, they gave me love and the best childhood a kid could want, and from those moments my imagination was born; Marsha for her support since day one years ago when I told her I wanted to be a writer, she never laughed at my dream and encouraged me all those early mornings; Johnathan Echeverria for believing enough to come out his own pockets; and finally, all of the friends and family who have supported me up to this point, the journey is just getting started.

I can't thank you enough for buying this book! If, after reading, you find that you enjoyed it, please leave a review on the site from which it was purchased. I'd love to hear what you think. Also, if you would like to be added to my email list for updates on new projects, cover art previews, and bios of new characters, please click below:

http://eepurl.com/coooRH

If you want to learn more about me, and witness my attempts at blogging:

www.rileytune.weebly.com

PROLOGUE

It happened again a few days ago.

A part of me feels like I'm going crazy; at the same time I can't help but be intrigued. If I believed in the Keeper, this would be the point at which I'd would pray to him and ask for guidance but I don't spend time worshiping mythical beings that I can't see.

I closed my eyes and allowed my head to tilt back. If my eyes had been open, I'd have been looking up directly into the evening sky. Instead, I kept them closed, and let the snow fall onto my face and melt. It felt good.

Today was a day that contained snow. That was how it was in Thera. Thera, like all the kingdoms in the Prime Sovereignty, had snow every day. And every night, without fail, the rain came to wash the snow away, and the cycle started all over again. This was the world I lived in. Snow and rain, snow and rain again. Day in and day out. It never froze, though. Even when it snowed, the warmth of the sun kept it from staying.

Horrible weather was the least of my problems, though. I was dealing with an internal battle of nerves. I had just turned fifteen, and by Thera standards, that meant that I could work, and held almost as much say in things as an adult. I wouldn't be ignored as a child anymore. This new-found responsibility wasn't really, well, exciting. It simply meant that I would have to find a job.

That's why I was here: standing outside this, building waiting for my mother to come outside.

She was supposed to see if the employers of this grow

shelter needed extra workers. If they did, then, hopefully, I would get the job. That would mean three incomes in the house instead of two, and we would finally be able to breathe a little.

I heard a door being opened from the interior of the grow shelter. This entire time I had been leaning on the building, facing the almost empty-streets of Thera. I turned around and looked into the building. It was large, by grow shelter standards, and the outer layer was made of mostly glass.

I couldn't really see inside the shelter. Instead, I saw a warped reflection of myself. I'll admit I looked a mess. I could see in my tall, lanky reflection that my black hair was sprinkled with snow. The same went for my brown trousers, and my shirt, once white, now gray. I stepped closer to the building, trying to see inside.

Leaning in, I clasped my hands around my eyes, and allowed them to touch the glass. It was cold against my skin, and grainy from the dirt that coated its surface.

I couldn't see the massive amount of crops being grown on the inside. That happened deeper inside the grow shelter, and this was only the entrance. What I could see was a woman walking toward me. As I had hoped, it was my mother. She was dressed in her normal work clothing—one piece, which covered her from her neck to her feet.

Her massive crop-attendant gloves made her hands look monstrous for a woman of her small stature. Her brown hair was in a tight ponytail, and she waved at me gently as she began to undo it. My mother hated—and I mean *hated*—wearing her hair in any way other than falling freely on her shoulders. She said it always made her hair feel like it was being held hostage.

I went ahead and opened the door for her so that she

could walk out onto the city street with me. The door was heavier than I expected and made a loud creaking sound as I slowly opened it. Immediately, snowflakes began to find a home in her hair.

"So, how did it go?" I asked her.

"I spoke to him. He just isn't looking for any more workers right now, sweetie. I'm sorry," she said, leaning on the building and looking around, avoiding eye contact with me. Her voiced cracked as she spoke.

Just as her voice betrayed her, so did her glossy eyes.

"It's okay, Mom. I'll stop by some local shops tomorrow and ask if anybody needs help," I said, pulling away from her.

"Maybe I could do metal work for the guards." I paused, thinking about it. No, that job would be horribly dangerous. The guards were well known for doing extreme things to the workers who messed up their orders. So that was out.

There was always work for a person who wanted to be a Torch Runner. Torch Runners were people who patrolled around a predetermined section of Thera, before the rain came each night, to light fires atop of large metal poles with their ends enclosed in glass. This glass would protect the flame from the rain, providing light to the city at night. This was one of the few jobs that were done the same way no matter which kingdom you lived in. It was simple work, but it was work nonetheless, and somebody had to do it.

My mom wouldn't want me doing that, either, I'm sure. So I didn't even bother mentioning it to her.

"I think the lady who works near the palace entrance could use some help."

My mother wiped her eyes. "What makes you say that?"

"Any time I walk by, it's only her working, and she always seems to have more customers than she can handle alone."

My mother raised a brow. She was seeing the glimmer of hope, no doubt. Hope that the fate most common for boys my age wouldn't happen to me.

But that's right; I was fifteen now. I was a man. She was worried about the fate of men my age. The fate of the Yolar Mines.

The Yolar Mines were mines located in every kingdom. The men worked them day after day to find the metals used to make currency for the Prime Sovereignty.

Yolars came in three different metals. Bronze, silver, and gold. Gold was the most common Yolar, and, as such, carried a lesser value than the others. Bronze was the most precious of the three.

The more valuable the metal, the harder it was to find, and the harder it was to mine. Naturally, because my luck was always the worst, the mines located in Thera were bronze mines. That meant longer hours and harder work to find the elusive metal.

I wasn't keen on becoming a mine worker. Many went in at fifteen and never saw the light of day again until they were well into their fifties. The irony of it all was that, for a job that literally found materials to turn into wealth, it paid less than any other industry. You only ended up in the mines if you had no other options. The mine bosses knew this and used it to their advantage.

"Head on home," my mom said, as she removed the excess snow from her hair and pulled it back into a tail again. "Nowrt should be there with the twins by now, and will likely need your help."

I nodded. Nowrt, my mother's current husband and

my stepfather, worked in a grow shelter too, but in a different area. He was a good guy. Better than my father had been, for sure. My father—I wouldn't have known him if he'd walked past me and waved and stuck his tongue out. He'd left my mother well before I could talk. At least that's what I'd always been told.

"I love you, Lox," she said, as she placed her hand on my face and ruffled my hair.

"Love you too, Mom," I said, with a smile.

Mothers were special that way. Here I was, a man now, who towered over her, and yet she still made me feel like a little boy. If she'd only known what was happening to me.

How would she react?

With her massive work gloves back on, she opened the door, and vanished back into the inner workings of the grow shelter. I clenched my jaw as I turned and faced the street once more.

There weren't many people walking during this time of day. Most of them, like my mother, were at work, and seeing as I didn't have a job, and had completed school like every other fifteen-year-old, I had time on my hands.

For the most part I was alone, except for a figure that was across the street. From the build, it was clearly a man. A well-built, solid man. I couldn't see his face, for he wore a cloak that covered most of his body, and the hood was up.

Smart, I thought to myself. It wasn't cold, but if I had had a way to keep the snow from continuously falling on my face, I would have used it too. A cloak wasn't my style, but it seemed to be working for him.

I could have been wrong, but was he looking at me, or the grow shelter behind me? I began to move a few feet in the direction of home. As I moved, the figure's head turned slightly and followed me.

He was definitely looking at me, and here came the nerves. I figured the best thing to do was to get moving and avoid not make eye contact, so I picked up my speed. I walked a few feet. In my mind I kept telling myself, *don't do it, don't do it*, but I couldn't help it, and I looked over my shoulder as I walked.

Sure enough, the figure was walking too.

"Stupid," I said to myself as I looked forward again. I was sure he had seen me look. I tried not to, I really did, but I looked in his direction once more. His black cloaked flapped a little behind him as he walked. His hands were drawn now, and he seemed to have on some sort of protective layer covering them. That was odd. Only guards wore armor of any kind.

My throat felt dry as his cloak moved slightly and revealed what was unmistakably the handle of a knife.

Carrying a knife in Thera wasn't uncommon; it was actually almost expected. But a man carrying a knife and following me was a bit of a bother. Against my better judgment, I looked over my shoulder across the street again to see if I was still being followed, and prepared myself to run like my feet were on fire.

I exhaled as I saw that I wasn't being followed anymore. I stopped mid-step and looked back toward the place the man had been in moments before. He was gone. I relaxed, turning back around.

I screamed as I walked directly into the cloaked man.

He was standing in front of me. I looked across the street to where he had been, and then back to him in front of me. I could feel my chest rising and falling rapidly. How had he gotten from behind me and across the street to in front of me that quickly, and without being seen? I could still run, I told myself. I was pretty fast.

I began to back away, but his hand shot out with such a speed that the snow falling around him was dispelled. His grip on my arm was strong. Too strong for me to break away.

"I know what you are, boy." His voice came from under the cloak. It was smooth, yet coarse.

"Know what I am?" I repeated, in shock, as I tried to remove his hand.

"I know what you are, and what you can do." He looked at me as his other hand removed the hood of his cloak. "And now, you belong to me."

PART I

1

For the following two years, I did in fact belong to him. On occasion, I would see my family again. I was happy that I was experiencing one of those occasions now. My mom placed four square plates on the table.

From where I sat in the living room it was easy to see almost all of our little house. There was the kitchen, currently almost empty. All of the brown cabinets were bare, and so was the icebox where we kept the meat.

In the middle of the kitchen was a small square table that had been in the family for years. It was almost as old as the plates.

It was worn, the legs wobbled, and the top was likely to give you splinters, but it served its purpose.

Then there was the living room. It was my personal favorite room, and where I was currently sitting, on the red rug. The same red rug that I could remember playing on as a child.

Once these rooms had seemed so cramped. My mom had shared with Nowrt, and I had to share with the twins. Now, things were different. Now, the twins slept in a room to themselves. Since I was unable to live here anymore, it provided them with plenty of space.

About a year ago, Nowrt had gotten a transfer to work in the grow shelter with my mom. Things had been great until the accident happened. Most of the people working in that area had lost their lives that day—Nowrt being one of them. My mom wasn't hurt physically, but it had done something to her. She hadn't been able to work since, and now she, too, had a room to herself.

"Luka, Kula!" she shouted through the house. "Come and eat." Even when she yelled at them, her voice was soft, and even though she didn't work, she always sounded like she was tired. Likely she was worried about me, and spent her time thinking about that.

I could hear the twins running from their room. They entered the kitchen in their favorite red sleeping clothes and, despite being almost time for bed, they were both full of energy. They both looked so much like my mother that it was scary. They both had her brown hair, and lots of it.

Luka, my brother, had her round eyes, and my sister Kula had her nose and her grin. I didn't see my mother use that grin much now, but I did remember it. They didn't have many of Nowrt's features, though. My mom used to joke that she hoped they would get his height. "As long as they aren't as short as me," she'd said. That was back when Nowrt was alive, and her joking and smiling was more common.

She began putting food on the plates. I didn't know what it was. It looked like chicken, or some sort of meat that I hoped was chicken. Whatever it was, it smelled good, and I was hungry. I pushed myself from the floor and stretched as I peered out the window. It had gotten dark outside. The snow had stopped about an hour ago, and the rain had begun to fall. I let out a sigh. My time was almost up, and I would be leaving soon.

"We still have some time," my mom said as she glanced at me and put the last pieces of food on the plate.

"Plenty of time," I said with a smile. I'm sure she could tell I was faking it. She always could.

I handled most of the family expenses now. I was seventeen, and had been working for two years. That was also why I didn't live here anymore. My job, if that's what you could call it, kept me away a lot. It was hard work that I really didn't enjoy doing, but my family needed me. My curse had become their gift, I supposed.

We all began eating and, as usual, the food was good. It actually was chicken. I enjoyed it—not just the food, but the family time, as well. I wished the time would go by more slowly. It would be an entire week before I got to see them again, maybe longer. We ate our food in silence at first; then Luka looked up at me from his plate. Sauce was spread over his face and all on his fingers. Even at seven, he preferred to eat with his hands.

"Want some?" he said as he grabbed a handful of food and extended it to me. I tried not to, but I could feel my lips parting in a smile. Between their natural innocence, and those little voices, almost everything the twins did was adorable.

"I can't eat yours, bud." I held up my food. "I got my own right here." He looked down at his plate, and then, unexpectedly, hurled the food at my sister.

Kula screamed as the food landed in her hair and fell to her almost-empty plate. She still had plenty to throw some back at him while screaming, "I can do that, too!" at the top of her lungs.

"Hey!" I yelled at them, to get them to stop. I began to stand up, but my mom placed her hand on my leg.

"Let them play. If it wasn't for cleaning up their messes, I'd die of boredom in this house." She smiled as she watched the food fight unfold.

"If you say so," I said as I picked my plate off the table, to eat my food without worrying about getting caught between them.

"They seem so normal, don't they?" she said, almost

absently.

"Are they not normal?" I asked, as I looked at her with my brow raised.

She shrugged. "Maybe." She paused for a second and let her eyes shift to me, but she didn't turn her head. She nudged me in the side. "Then again, you seemed normal at that age, too, and look at you now."

I cleared my throat. "Oh." That was all I could say. As she sat there in her night clothes, I couldn't help but think she had a point. We looked at each other for a moment that seemed to last too long. "I'm sure—"

Before I could finish my words, the air in the living room shimmered out of focus for a second. My mother didn't notice it, but I had more experience with what was happening than she did.

In an instant, a man popped into existence, and began to remove his black cloak.

Luka and Kula stopped their fighting and ran to the man in the living room. "Ember!" they shouted as they got closer to him.

He said nothing, but the grimace on his face was enough.

"Room. Now," my mom said as she stood from the table and pointed to the back portion of the house.

"Get that look off of your face. They're just kids," I said to the man.

He folded his cloak evenly over his arm, then placed it on a chair in the living room. The same cloak he had been wearing that day we'd first met, two years ago, near my mother's grow shelter job. Ember was scary to the core, and I'm not just saying that because of the way he acted.

He was a tall man with dark skin. He was in his mid-forties, but he still had considerable muscle tone and an inhumanly muscular chest. Likely a result of the line of work we were in.

His scruffy beard and black hair were of a woolen texture, and he had tattoos from the base of his neck down his upper body that were barely visible. Yes, he was an imposing man; and even after all this time, he still sometimes scared me as much as he had that first day.

"Ember," my mother said with a fake smile as she slid her plate towards him. "You may as well eat before you take my son away from me again."

"Thank you," Ember said as he vanished into thin air and reappeared beside the table. My mother jumped a little. I rolled my eyes and sipped my water.

"Would you stop? You warped all of five feet," I said, looking at him with a grin as he sat down.

"Remember who the teacher is here, boy," he replied as he began to eat.

My mom stood from the table as she removed the twin's plates. She didn't mind Ember, but she could only tolerate him in small doses. I'm not sure if it was because of what he was, or if it's because of what he did.

I should say it was because of what we *were*. Ember, for all his rugged glory, was just like me. We were both born with this same curse. The curse that had frightened me when I was fifteen to the point that I couldn't bear to tell my own mother.

We were both killers. We were both Warpers. The rarest of Warpers. People able to move long distances in the span of a heartbeat. I could be standing here one moment, and in the twins' room the next. As long as our destination was in our line of site, we could warp there.

There were other Warpers out there. Not many were inward Warpers, like Ember and I, but there were a good

21

amount of outward Warpers. People able to warp objects to and from them, but not to warp themselves.

This wasn't the curse, though. The curse was what inward Warpers *were:* assassins. Ember, who for the last two years had served as my teacher, says that, since the dawn of time, Warpers were blessed by the Keeper. Blessed to be able to move like we do, blessed to mold history with a slash of our blades, and blessed to take life.

That was our curse. Did I honestly believe that Warpers had been doing this from the dawn of time? Not even a little. I knew we were forced to take lives even when we didn't want to. To keep the balance. My saving grace was that the curse didn't take effect until you actually fulfilled your first contract.

If you never kill a person, then you can continue to warp without consequence. But once you take a life, it starts. From that moment on, you are destined to continue killing in some form or fashion. If we didn't, then our ability to warp would fade. Could I simply stop now? Yes. I would remain a Warper and keep all of my abilities. The thought of this sat fine with me, but I had to consider my family. This was the only source of income my family had, and assassination paid pretty well.

"Do you two need anything for the road? There is a little food left," Mom said, as she moved around the kitchen cleaning.

"No, I think we're good," I said, as I stood from the table. A small bag hit me in the chest. I caught it and looked at Ember, who was standing and checking his throwing knives.

"For Beckton and Venzor," he said casually as he began to adjust the leather greaves on his lower leg.

I opened the small bag and looked inside. There were

two gold yolars, and a handful of silver yolars. The small coins in this bag could support my family for a month. Knowing my mother, she'd buy food for a week or two and then give the rest to people she owed money to in Thera.

It was a good payday for very little work done on my part. Actually, no work had been done on my part. Not yet. Between the two of us, Ember was the master. Some believed him to be one of the most dangerous men in all the Prime Sovereignty.

As a Warper, you were eventually drawn to another Warper as their powers developed. This was how Ember had found me on the street that day. As I learned from him, I'd get small paydays like this, until I was ready to carry out assassinations of my own. Luckily, that day was far off. I wasn't ready to take a life yet, and Ember knew it. Demanding as he was, I was thankful for the patience he had with me.

I removed three of the silver yolars and gave the rest of the bag to my mom. She looked inside the bag and then at me. Once she would have fought taking the bag. She hated what we did to make our money, but she had the twins to think about. Food was running out, and we didn't know when our next contract would come.

"Lox," she said with a sigh as she placed the bag on the table and gave me a hug, "you are more a man that your father ever was." Her arms tightened around me once more, and then relaxed. "Be safe out there." She handed me a large bag.

It was my bag. The bag I always used when I came home. It was time to go.

I opened the bag slowly and found the tools of my craft. She kept it hidden from the twins when I came home to visit. She didn't want them to know my secret just yet.

They knew what I could do, but not why.

I removed my greaves first and I dropped down to place them on my lower leg. They were made of a strong leather that offered protection and still allowed us to move with ease. Next came my bracers. They were just like the bracers worn by Ember, who was now leaning on the wall, breathing heavy. He rolled his eyes and allowed his finger to drum against his leg.

I clasped my bracers to my arms. After that I put on my belt. It was a belt we had to have made specially so that it could hold our weapons. Ember and I both carried similar knives. His knives were better, of course. We both had three throwing knives that were solid black steel.

They were double sided and had a small hole in the handle. The hole allowed it to keep perfect balance as it was thrown. I ran my finger along the edge of the little knife gently. It truly was a work of art.

Knives were my thing. Something about them, the way they felt in my hand, the way they looked, always fascinated me. These were my main knives, but I had recently decided to start a collection of my own, like Ember had.

In his time, Ember had collected everything from rare swords wielded by kings to daggers used by warriors of legend. He kept them as reminders of his kills, but I would keep them for their beauty.

Naturally Ember was better with his blades than I was with mine, but I was learning.

"Would you hurry up?" Ember bellowed at me. I paid him no attention. For the most part he was all show. Even if he did want to hurt me, which I'm almost positive he didn't, he likely wouldn't. Inward Warpers were too rare. Before me, it had been a decade since he'd met another new one.

As his arms crossed I could see his dagger on his belt.

The dagger we used was much larger than our throwing knives. Made of mostly steel, with a black leather handle, it was the go-to weapon for a Warper. Unlike Ember, who had two daggers, I only had the one. I wasn't skilled enough to wield two yet.

I finally put on my cloak. "I'm ready," I said to him as he began to open the front door. Instantly the sound of the falling rain poured into the room.

"Shorn. As always, it's been a pleasure," he said as he looked at my mom.

"Keep him safe, Ember," she said to him.

He didn't reply, but he gave a half-smile and a nod. He put up his hood, took a step, letting his foot pass over the entrance to the house, and then vanished.

"I'll be fine, Mom," I said as I approached the door.

The twins came running back in the room. Clearly they couldn't stand being left out anymore, and they both embraced my mother around her legs. Those three were my world. I was the man of the house, and I had to provide.

Everything—no, everyone—depended on me.

I put my hood up and turned from them and looked out the door. The rain was coming down hard, but the torch runner had already come, so even with the added darkness, it was still easy to see. Ember was standing on top of a building across the street, waiting for me.

I took a deep breath and reached inside of myself. Touching that unknown yet unmistakable energy. It was harmony. It was power. And it was mine. The sound from the rain falling down around me faded, and for a moment all was quiet. I let my breath go and I warped.

2

Reappearing beside Ember on top of the building, I had to reposition my cloak hood to keep the rain from splattering against my face. I turned slightly to look over my shoulder and glanced at my house once more.

"I miss them already," I said as a flickering light from the small house went out.

"Nonsense," Ember said, smacking me on the upper part of my back, a little too hard. "You will be back in no time."

I nodded. "Let's hope the week goes by fast, then," I said.

Ember turned away from me quickly. Was this by chance, or was he avoiding eye contact? "Everything okay?" I asked him. He snorted in reply.

"Depends on how you see things," he finally said.

"I trust you know where the first statue of the Emperor is?" He had to yell a little to be heard over the rain.

"Who doesn't know where that is?" I replied.

"Good. Meet me there."

I turned my face up as I watched him turn in the general direction of the main statue. In seconds he had warped, and left me standing there alone on the roof top.

This wasn't at all how our training sessions started. Usually we spent time either going over hand to hand combat, knife defense or offense, or warping without being seen. It had always been this way for most of the two years I had been learning from him. It only changed when we had a contract or had to scout.

"A contract," I said out loud in surprise. That must have been why we weren't training. Odd for us to land one so quickly after the last.

Even more curious was that Ember hadn't told me about it yet. Murder must have been booming right now in the Kingdom. People always assumed that brothels and sex were the Prime Sovereignty's oldest profession, but I knew better. Murder. That was it.

If this was a contract, I knew I had better get moving and catch up to Ember to learn as much as I could. He already had a considerable lead over me. Finding him wasn't going to be an issue, though. That was how our Warper Bond worked. When an older, more experienced Warper was suddenly drawn to a new Warper, the bond was created.

We didn't know why it worked this way, but Ember thought it was to ensure that skills were always passed down from teacher to student. To ensure no lines were crossed. Like assassinating a King, or somebody important for no reason.

So even though Ember was gone, if I focused, I could kind of feel where his general presence was. It was weird, but it worked. After I'd learned what I was, I'd pretty much stopped questioning the weird and simply believed in what I saw or felt.

I focused for a moment, and in an instant, I could feel something inside me pulling towards a certain direction. I turned and looked out on the endless rows of buildings and houses. Setting my eyes on the highest one I could see, I ran and warped to it.

Warping is a unique sensation. You can literally feel it inside you. A brief, short tingle of sorts, right before it happens. After that, for a moment, there is complete silence, and you vanish from one spot and reappear into another.

I used to actually wonder where we went for that second in which we disappeared. We had to go someplace before we popped into another. That was one of the few question I'd asked that Ember didn't have an answer for. He was one of the oldest Warpers alive, and even he didn't know. So I just let it go. If he didn't know, I assumed it really didn't matter.

Standing on this building now, I could see so much of Thera. Even in the pouring rain, it was truly a beautiful city. Of all the kingdoms, this was the nicest in the Prime Sovereignty by far, but this was likely due to the fact that the Emperor himself ruled over Thera personally. Many of the buildings, like my home, were small and built without a lot of thought. Just some rooms to sleep in, a kitchen, and a wash room. Other buildings, however, were marvels. Some, like the one I was standing on now, had as many as three levels, and were built to last.

As you got closer to the palace, buildings changed drastically. The closer to the palace you got, the closer you got to nobility and the wealthy.

The homes there were made out of iron and stone, not wood and clay. They grew as high as four floors, and very few of the lower classes actually got a chance to see inside of them.

I took in the view of the city through the rain once more and kept moving. Ember was surely fuming at me now for being late.

I warped a few more times in the same direction until the main statue of the Emperor came into view. It was tall and looked identical to the Emperor in all of his glory.

There were many statues of the Emperor, and his descendants, throughout the Prime Sovereignty, but this one was different. This statue was called the first one because it was made completely out of bronze, making the statue itself worth a fortune. Its location had become something of legend for many and a holy spot for others.

Lord of Thera and all kingdoms of the Prime Sovereignty, Emperor Anavor Nal, had declared this spot to be the location of this statue, and ordered that this statue be different from the rest because this very spot was the first place that he had died. It was also where the world had learned that Emperor Nal could rise from the dead. It took time, but he did indeed come back.

Since then, he had died numerous times in one way or another, and he had always returned. The Emperor, much like Ember and myself, seemed to be able to do something that other people could not. Death would try to claim him, and in a day's time he would always return.

"Hey!" A voice came from the shadows and caused me to jump slightly.

I turned and saw Ember standing behind me. "What took you so long? I thought somebody'd finally come along and killed you. I thought I was free of this damn bond for a moment."

I said nothing. He caught his breath as he looked at me, waiting for me to laugh.

"You didn't think that was funny? I thought it was funny."

Since the day we'd met, I'd known Ember was a unique individual. He spent most of his time alone, and other times, he was taking the life of another. Needless to say, he was a grim person. I'd told him he needed to relax some. Learn to laugh and joke like a normal person.

The problem was that Ember just didn't get how jokes worked, for some reason. Even when he was trying to joke, it always came out wrong, and was usually laced with violence.

"It wasn't funny, but at least you're trying," I said as I looked around. "Why are we here?"

He gathered himself and put on his normal passive face again. "New contract," he said as he walked over and jumped off the building. I rolled my eyes and followed.

I glanced over the edge of the building and saw him standing three floors below. I jumped and warped slightly in the air to the ground—otherwise the jump would have likely left me with broken legs. The ground was softer from the rain, but not soft enough to help in a fall.

"What new contract?" I asked.

Ember said nothing, but he did smile. This scared me more than anything.

"Ember?" I asked. "What's going on?"

"Tonight is your night," he said calmly.

"My night for what?"

"This contract is yours," he said as he moved from the building and began walking. I froze for a second. Surely he didn't mean *mine*. This wasn't how it worked. I learned, I observed, I didn't do contracts. Not yet. I couldn't.

I didn't know which scared me more. The thought of having to kill, or knowing that, because of this curse, once I started, I wouldn't be able to stop.

"Ember!" I said as I began to move. "What are you talking about?" I ran to catch up to him, splashing through puddles of rainwater that were in my way. He kept walking, seemingly oblivious to me. "Ember!"

He stopped walking instantly. I had shouted at him. I'd shouted at him as if he was a child running through the city streets unattended. I swallowed down the lump in my throat. He turned and looked at me. He was taller than me, and from this angle his eyes seemed to blaze from under his hood. I realized that yelling at him may not have been the best idea. As the rain fell down around us, the streets seemed oddly quiet. I avoided his gaze.

"Sorry," I said finally. The tension in his body relaxed some as he continued to walk, at a slower pace.

"Follow me," he said gruffly as he moved. I did. We turned from the side street and found ourselves walking on one of the main streets in Thera. This street was considerably more busy.

Many people, not just Ember and I, were walking tonight, despite the heavy rain. It was evident that we were in a nicer, more upper-class portion of the city. Everything from the buildings to the clothes people wore shouted wealth. Most of the people on the street had special clothing on that repelled the rain. Nobody I knew could ever afford such an article of clothing. While many walked, there were some that rode what was being called a bicycle.

This bicycle invention was an oddity. It was said to be an invention by a man in the Walden kingdom. It was made with an iron frame and had large wheels on each end. They were different from what was usually seen on carriages. They were smaller, and made out of something other than wood. This was the closest I'd ever been to one.

Only the high nobility could afford something as expensive as a bicycle. Normal nobility could afford servants, and carriages, but to have a bicycle you had to either belong to a royal family, or have a lot of yolars to spend.

I continued to follow Ember and tired not to gawk every time a person rode a bicycle past us. High noble or not, they looked ridiculous riding those things in the rain. Ember had slowed down a little more to the point that I had to will myself to walk more slowly.

"Up there, in the dark overcoat and hat. Do you see him? The one with the cane."

I nodded my head as we continued to walk slowly.

"That is Lord Avery Ashland." My stomach began to twist as Ember said the words.

"Ashland?" I asked him. "The family that own the yolar mines and the torch runners?"

"Of course, that family."

I didn't reply as Ember continued.

"Lord Ashland has a very profitable contract on himself."

We followed Ashland down another street.

"Why?" I asked. Ember eyed me. It's normal practice not to question the contract. Somebody wanted him dead, and wanted to pay us to do it. That was all that I needed to know. I knew Ember, though; he would have found out why such an important person was in our midst tonight.

"Lord Ashland has a fondness for the women of Vinc's brothels. He's actually on his way there now." This didn't seem odd to me at all. I wasn't one to agree with brothels, but it certainly didn't seem like something a contract would be put out for.

"So?" I asked as Ember paused.

"Lord Ashland not only has a fondness for women. He gets Vinc to procure women of a very young age. Once Lord Ashland has had his way with these women, he cuts them up in—unique ways. He stretches out the event to add to their suffering. Several have died, and a few have killed themselves, unable to cope with the event."

We kept walking, keeping Ashland in our view as he went. My feeling of reluctance vanished. If what Ember had said was true, this man certainly deserved to die. I just would have preferred not to be the one to do it. I loved being a Warper; I just hated the killing part of it.

"The hard work has been done for you," Ember said to me as he stepped off the main street and into a dark alley. "I have scouted this already, and I know exactly which roads he will take to get there. Because of his status, he goes out of his way not to be seen.

Shortly he will turn down another side street, and once on that street he will cut down a side walkway between two buildings. This is where you will strike. Light from the torch runners' flame will not shine there, and you will use the darkness and rain to your advantage. There will be just enough moonlight for you to see."

I looked around the street. I'm not sure why I was even looking; I just was too nervous to stay still. "I don't think I'm ready yet."

Ember adjusted his hood. "You are. Don't worry, I'll be watching. At the very worst, he attacks you first, and you die in a gutter," he said, with a wide grin. His grin faded just as quickly.

Before I could protest more, he warped away, leaving a faint shimmer in the air as he left.

"Dammit," I said under my breath. *Okay, Lox, you can do this. You've seen Ember do this a dozen times.*

First I needed to check my belt. My knives were all there, and so was my dagger. I warped to the top of the building along the street and began to run. In what seemed like no time, I'd caught up with Ashland. Just as Ember had said, he was turning down a side alleyway.

He had a smirk on his face, and as soon as he was alone, he started to spin his cane around, and did a little dance as he whistled a peculiar tune. I can only assume he was growing more excited as he approached his destination.

Here we go. Now or never. He was in the middle of the alley now. I took a deep breath and warped from the top of the building, appearing directly in front of Ashland. As I locked eyes with him I noticed the look of shock on his face. That same look was replaced with fear seconds later.

"No. Stay back," he said as he stepped away. Clearly Ashland knew what I was, and if he was seeing me, he knew what I had come to do. He was a young man, no more than twenty-five, and had boyish features. His face was smooth, and his eyes seemed too far apart. Like others of his wealth, his overcoat repelled the water that fell on it.

"You don't have to do this." Ashland said. "I have money!"

His begging angered me. "Do the children you cut and disfigure beg you not to do it?" I asked calmly, not letting my anger show. I needed to make this fast. Wherever he was, Ember was watching, and he hated slow kills. The rain had begun to fall more slowly now. He continued to back away from me. Was he really trying to leave?

Indeed he was. At that very moment, he turned to run towards the entrance of the alley. I rolled my eyes and warped again, this time appearing in front of him and in his way. He seemed to be so set on running that he had forgotten what I could do. I delivered a punch to his stomach that sent him to the ground in the mud. His fancy coat couldn't repel that.

He cried out and grabbed his stomach. I stood over him and reached for my dagger. As I pulled it out from under my cloak I heard Ashland gasp for air. This wasn't a gasp from pain. This was terror leaving his body.

I leaned in and grabbed his throat. His eyes grew wide as he struggled, clawing at me with his free hand as his cane jerked in the other.

Strength-wise, Ashland may have been stronger than me. He certainly was larger, but over the last two years I had learned that fear made men weak. I placed my knife at his throat, and even with the small amount of pressure I had applied, blood still began to drip. I couldn't believe I was doing this. If I went through with it, it would start. The curse would begin and I would not, could not, stop.

For the rest of my life, I would be forced to take the life of others. Could I live with that? Did I even have a choice?

"Please," Ashland pleaded.

My steady hand began to shake. *Pull it together*, I said to myself. *This is who you are.* The shaking in my hand seemed to increase and, for a second, my grip on Ashland's neck gave way.

That second was all it took, and suddenly I felt a crushing blow to my head as I stumbled back. Ashland had hit me with his cane. I positioned myself.

"You don't seem to have the heart for this, boy," he said to me. *Who was this guy?* I thought. Then Ashland smoothly removed the handle end of his cane, revealing a slender blade on the end. It was a nice blade, too. Polished steel, with some sort of writing etched in the side. A blade befitting his noble status in Thera.

"Myself, I have no problem cutting," Ashland said. "It's something about the feeling of flesh parting that is—" He paused, searching for the right words. "*Blissful* to me." With those final words, he lunged at me.

3

Ashland had the eyes of a madman as he came crashing down with his nobleman's blade. Naturally, his attack was pointless. He may have been noble and wealthy, but he wasn't quick enough to get the drop on a Warper. Seconds before he could land on me, I warped to a position directly behind him. He turned quickly on me. His brown hair was messy now, and looked more like that of a wild man instead of a noble. His hat had long since fallen.

This was bad, I thought to myself, as Ashland's grip tightened on his blade handle. It popped into my head again that Ember was watching, and I'm pretty sure he was upset. I'd bet my dagger on it. I had Ashland. His life was in my hands, and I froze. That wasn't the Warper way. Now I would have to make this right.

Holding my dagger in one hand, I quickly drew one of my three throwing knives with my other. In my first days of training, the knife would slip from my hands as a result of sweat and rain on my palms. Not now, though.

It made a whistling sound as it ripped through the air and plunged into Ashland's shoulder. He screamed out in pain and instantly dropped his blade to the ground, using that hand to cover the wound. I smiled for a second. He wasn't used to fighting, that was for sure.

"Hey!" a voice shouted out. My head jerked so hard towards the noise that my hood fell. The sudden increase of rain flooded into my eyes and caused my hair to cling to my head. "What are you doing down there?"

Guards. Three of them. They must have heard Ashland's scream.

In an upper-class part of Thera like this, guards made rounds pretty frequently. They approached slowly, all dressed exactly alike in lightweight suits of armor that reflected the moonlight onto to the walls of buildings in the alley. They looked almost as if they were glowing.

The guard in the front had on a helmet that left his face exposed, but most of his head protected. He was a dark-skinned man, with a wide forehead and eyebrows as thick as my finger. He let his hand rest on the end of his sword gently, but his posture was stern and rigid.

"Lord Ashland, is that you?" the guard in the front said as he leaned closer and drew his sword. Great. Of course they knew each other. That was how my luck worked.

"He's a Warper!" Ashland said as he ran towards the guard. "He's trying to kill me." He pointed to the wound on his neck, continuing to hold his bleeding shoulder as he ran and screamed. "You will be paid double your wages in yolars—just kill him. Kill him now!"

Without warning a spear broke through the darkness and buried itself into the wall directly behind me. Now this guard was left defenseless. Not too bright at all.

Had I not been ready to warp, the spear would have easily found its mark between my shoulders. I needed to get out of here, and fast. Too many witnesses, too much of everything. Everything was going wrong in such a short amount of time. I saw Ashland finally making his way behind the guard. He stood for a second and looked in my direction. Then he ran. In those seconds, those brief moments, my entire purpose for being here was gone. I had failed.

Suddenly, the alley around me went black. I struggled,

trying to remove whatever was over my head, but I couldn't. It felt like some sort of sack. Whatever it was, it had an odor that you could smell two kingdoms away. Somebody had entered the alley from the other side, and I hadn't even heard them approaching. Whatever this was on my head, it left me unable to see, and because of that I couldn't warp away. I slashed out with my dagger, trying to hit something, anything, but I couldn't. The person holding the sack over my head was strong.

I felt a punch to my side and a kick to the back of my legs that dropped me to the ground. I caught myself as my knee began to throb. My hand was submerged in water now. I must have found a puddle as I'd fallen.

"We take him to the palace," said a voice that seemed to squeaky to be a man's.

My heart began to drum faster in my chest. The palace? Why take me there? Criminals usually were taken to the holding cells in the council building. Then again, I was no normal criminal. I was a Warper, and certain precautions were needed.

A muffled screamed pierced the air and the grip on my visual prison relaxed. I heard a loud thud beside me as the thing on my face fell loose. I removed it quickly to see a guard lying on the ground, looking directly at me. He had on no helmet and, while his body was lifeless, his eyes remained open. The blood flowing from his throat began to swirl as the falling rain mixed with it.

At the other end of the alley I saw him, moving with a speed that, even if I tried, I could never match. Ember had finally decided to step in. It had certainly taken him long enough.

His fluid motions, perfected over years of being a Warper, made him look like he was dancing. Like he had a rhythm to the way he delivered slashes from his dagger and blows from his fist. One of the guards who held a spear was already on the ground, dead. I could feel my eyes widen a little as my head jerked. I knew he was moving fast, but I hadn't even seen him attack that one. It was the one who had thrown his weapon at me. That made sense. Take out the weaker one first. He posed the least amount of a threat.

The second guard with a spear thrust it at Ember at the same time as a lead guard slashed with his sword. Ember warped, only slightly, to the side of the lead guard, slashing at the back of his leg. He spun so fast that his cloak flew up in his wake, and he slashed again at the opposite leg. The guard screamed and spat as his head jerked back and he stumbled to the ground. Ember's dagger found its mark both times in the one spot that the armor didn't cover.

The butt of the spear swung at Ember's face, but he dodged it, and at the same time, he threw one of his knives at the guard, instantly warping away. As the knife impaled the guard's throat, Ember appeared beside him and ripped the knife away, letting the guard fall. His spear made a loud clang as it fell from his hands and rolled away.

To his credit, the lead guard was still trying to swing at Ember with his sword, but with no legs to stand on, it was a futile attempt. One that looked almost comical. I moved a few feet closer as Ember warped behind him. He removed the guard's helmet and planted his knee to the side of the guard's head, and the guard fell face first on the ground. He wouldn't kill the last guard. That wasn't Ember's style.

While Ember was famous, almost legendary, even, as a Warper of extreme skill, he preferred to be feared. He thought fear traveled through the kingdoms of the Prime Sovereignty much faster than any other emotion. Killing all but one of the guards left one to tell the story to others.

When it was all over, he scowled at me as he placed his hood back on. I took a deep breath and swallowed the little bite of pride I had left.

"I'll see you at home." That was all he said in a gruff voice as he turned and warped away.

I stood silently for a moment. Motionless, I let the rain wash over me as it fell. The remaining guard had limped away, but I was pretty sure he would return with help. If nothing else to remove the three bodies of his fallen fellow guards. I put my dagger and throwing knife away. How had I let this happen? The way I saw it, if it wasn't for this damn curse looming over me, I wouldn't have hesitated. I wouldn't have frozen up the way I had. It truly wasn't my fault. Ashland would be dead, the contract would be completed, and Thera would likely be a better place without him.

I wanted to scream as I stood there in the alley. Instead, I slammed my hand against the side of a building repeatedly. My hand, vulnerable as it was, started to feel the pain immediately. Rubbing it, I decided it would be best to leave the alley. I didn't want to still be around when those guards returned.

Warping would have been the easier way, and it would have been a lot faster, too. Despite that, I opted to walk instead. Inside I couldn't help but think that, had I done what I needed to, all this could have been avoided. Those guards wouldn't have had to die, and Ember wouldn't have wasted these last two years of training.

As I walked I tried to convince myself over and over again that what had happened, or hadn't happened, wasn't my fault. I was wrong, though. Hate it as I might have, it was my fault. I had the chance, and I'd let it slip away.

I felt ashamed. I felt like every person walking around

me on the street was giving me side glances. As if they knew of my recent failure, and what I was.

I would have bet Ashland was currently telling his friends some glorious story of how he'd fought off a Warper in an alley. No doubt he had left out the part of my hesitation, and that his success was due to my faults. I couldn't let this happen again. Who knew what Ember would do when I got home?

Would he stop being my teacher? Could he even stop? I wasn't sure if the bond worked that way. Maybe the time I was taking to walk there would give him time to relax. Maybe he wasn't even upset. Maybe I had been imagining that look of disappointment on his face.

No, Lox Norcross, I thought, *you were not imagining it at all.* It was there. The look of disgust, and it was aimed at me.

I looked up around me. I was pretty close to Ember's place. He had many houses, of sorts, around the Prime Sovereignty. Some were so nice that you'd think a noble lived there. Others, like the one I was headed to, were more unappealing.

The closer I got to the house, the more I began to think of what would happen next. The only clear point of action was to perform the job. To kill Ashland, and execute the contract. This would likely be harder than expected. Ashland, assuming he was smart, would have guards with him at all times now when he entered the city.

Finally I found myself standing in front of Ember's place. It was different than most homes in Thera, and it was very hard to find unless you knew where to look. This wasn't by chance. Ember had gone out of his way to make his home hard to find. It also had no doors on the bottom floor, and the only windows it had were on the second floor.

The design was of his own imagining and was intended so that only Warpers had access to the house, and entry could only be gained by warping to the roof and using the door found there.

I warped to the top of the house. There it was. A lonely panel on the roof that led inside. It almost looked like a trap door.

Behind this door would be a small steep flight of stairs. I dropped down to my knee and for the last time vowed to myself that I would make this right. If not now, then as soon as possible.

My hand clasped around the handle, and I pulled it open. It made noise, and a lot of it. I slipped into the door and down the steps as fast as I could, so that too much rain wouldn't fall inside.

I closed my eyes for a second, and descended the final steps cautiously as I prepared to face whatever Ember had to throw at me.

4

I removed my cloak, bracers, and greaves and set them neatly on the floor. Ember's home, or at least this one, was full of potential that he wasted. If this home had belonged to my mother, or almost anybody besides Ember, it would look more homely. Instead, most of the rooms were empty. In the main room were two areas set up for sleeping. One for me, one for him. We didn't have beds, just places we slept on the floor.

There was a kitchen, but no table or chairs. He didn't keep much food around, either. Part of our training was that we were not allowed to eat every day in order to prepare us for a time when a contract might take us away from consistent meals. We usually ate once every other day, and before a job.

This was one more reason, as if I needed more, that I loved visiting my family. My mother didn't care much about Warper training, so if I came by, we ate. It wasn't always grand, but it was food.

What his home did have was candles. Lots and lots of candles. Ember seemed to love candles the same way I loved blades. He never told me what his obsession was with candles, but this house had thirty of them easily. With so many candles in one place, the walls always seemed like they were bouncing, which at times made my head and eyes hurt.

Ember was on his makeshift bed on the floor, carving at a chunk of wood with a knife.

He eyed me for a second and then went back to his

carving. I'd expected loud screams, hurtful words, and cold stares. What I was getting instead was silence, and it was more uncomfortable than the outrage I had prepared for.

I sat down on my sleeping area. Ember's knife stopped moving on his chunk of wood. What was he carving? I couldn't make out the figure.

From behind Ember slowly walked a short, wide, solid dog.

"Hey, Sprits," I said as he shook himself and trotted over to me.

Sprits was Ember's hound, and had been the only constant thing in his life until he found me. Sprits was a little over seven years old, stood less than two feet off the ground, and had wide brown eyes, a short stump of a tail, and rolls of fat skin.

In no time he was on his hind legs, licking me. Sprits had earned his name because, as a pup, and even now, he had a very bad problem with holding his water. According to Ember, the name had started as a joke, but eventually stuck.

"For Keeper's sake, Sprits, you traitor, get over here," Ember bellowed. Sprits listened and instantly stopped licking me, slowly walking to Ember. He walked in a circle a few times before sitting down.

"What happened today?" Ember said finally.

"I hesitated," I replied.

"No, you didn't. I saw you. I saw your posture; your hand was shaking harder than a leaf under the night's rain."

"It's just—" I began, but he held up a hand to stop me from talking.

"You know how old I was when I first killed a person and took on the curse?"

I nodded. I did know; he had told me plenty of times. Most Warpers don't find out what they are until around the age of fifteen, like me. Ember was different, though. He'd started warping at ten, and by time his teacher had come along, he had already had a good understanding of what he could do.

"You were twelve," I said slowly.

"By the time I was your age I was feared in most of the five kingdoms. Galcon, Kameace, Walden, Thera, and Pradeep—all had stories of things I had done." He took a deep breath. "Lox, this-this is what we are."

Ember began to spin the knife in his hand and then threw it at the wall, allowing it to make a loud thumping sound as it stuck.

"And that is what we do. We kill. Hell, you can even consider it as keeping the balance if it makes you feel better. The faster you accept who you are, the easier it will become. There may come a time when I will not be there to force my hand because yours is too shaky. Even Warpers can't cheat death forever."

I sat silent. I had never really considered the obvious— that one day I may be out here alone. Ember had done so much, and seen so much, that I honestly had just assumed he would always be there.

"Now run your drills and then turn in," he said as he got under his blankets, adjusted the pillow, and pulled Sprits in close with one hand. He always slept with a dagger in hand. "We have a big day tomorrow."

I wanted to talk more, but he had already turned, his back to me. The conversation was over, and in no time he would be asleep. I really didn't want to run my drills tonight, not after the night I had already had, but I did as I was told. I was already comfortable on my sleeping area, and my eyes had started to feel a little heavy, but I forced myself up and started putting back on my bracers and my greaves. Once I was dressed, again, I shifted my attention to the large wooden dummy in the corner.

It was a unique piece of training equipment with a body almost entirely of wood. Two sections of the body near the top were wrapped completely in padding, and so was a small portion at the bottom. Up top were various smaller portions of wood that protruded out to represent limbs. Here I would run through various combinations of blocking, kicking and striking.

Ember had told me that most Warpers really didn't care how the kill was done, as long as it was done. He didn't do things that way. He preferred to practice one killing blow a thousand times instead of doing a thousand killing blows one time. So if possible, regardless of the combination, he taught me to always allow my blade to find the throat. That was usually how he killed. Always the throat.

I ran my drills time and time again until my limbs were sore. By the time I was done, my shoulders were on fire, my back was stiff, and my shins hurt, even with the protective greaves on. I may not have been ready to kill yet, but I could certainly hold my own in a fight. Sweaty, sticky and downright tired, I removed all of my clothing and got into my sleeping area. I could always bathe when I woke up; I didn't smell that bad. I checked to make sure my dagger was in reaching distance and closed my eyes.

5

Whack.

Pain shot across my face as my eyes jerked open. I grabbed my dagger and warped to the first area I saw. My back faced the wall, and my dagger was raised in case I had to attack.

"Good reflexes, but it's just me," Ember said.

"What?" I asked as I rubbed sleep from my eyes, dagger still in hand. "And why did you hit me so hard?"

He tossed me a chunk of bread.

"Thanks.

How long you been up?" I asked between chewing mouthfuls.

"Long enough. Snow's been falling for a while now. Figured I'd let you sleep a little longer, considering the night you had."

I nodded as I continued to chew.

"Wash up and then get dressed. I can smell you from here," he said.

He gave Sprits a large chunk of bread that he removed from a pocket under his cloak. The hound quickly grabbed the bread and trotted off to eat in a corner. Ember wiped the remaining crumbs from his hands.

"Meet me on the roof when you're done, and be quick about it. Keeper knows we don't have time to waste today."

That was one thing about Ember that I hated, and I mean *really* hated. As smart as he was and as deadly as he was, he, like almost all people in Thera and across the kingdoms in The Prime Sovereignty, insisted on believing in the Keeper. A god that supposedly watched over us. I thought differently. If I couldn't see it, or it couldn't be proved to me, then I didn't believe it. I had always been this way, and not many people thought as I did. Their belief was one of the few things my mom and Ember agreed on.

To hear Ember tell it, our ability to warp was a gift from the Keeper, and we should believe more than others, but I didn't. I also didn't voice it as much as I wanted to. My belief shouldn't have an effect on anybody else, and for the most part, I didn't let theirs affect me.

He warped away to an upper level of the house and began walking towards the stairs that led to the roof door. Sunlight shone in as he opened it. Sprits came over to me and leaned on my leg. He had finished his bread and likely wanted to play.

I gave a final rub to the top of his head and got going.

The first thing I did was gather my things. I used the wash room, got dressed, and then finished my bread. In what seemed like record time I was on my way to join Ember on the roof. The warmth of the sun radiated on my skin as soon as I stood outside.

Like many mornings in Thera, the mixture of falling snow and sunshine provided a beautiful landscape. I preferred the snowy days much more than the rainy nights, even though most of my time was dedicated to working at night. The nature of the job, I supposed.

"So what's this big day all about?" I asked as I stood beside him.

"Not here," he said as he pointed to a tall four-story building nearby. "There," he said, and then he warped away.

I exhaled, wondering why he couldn't stop being dramatic for just a second, and then I followed, allowing my world to go silent as I warped away and reappeared beside him.

The view from here was a hundred times better than that from the top of Ember's home. We could see the city on all sides now. People walked by, busy with their day-to-day activities. Carriages rushed down street, pulled by caprongs. Beast that stood taller than a horse, with large muscles covered by silky fur, and a head that resembled a wolf.

"I have been thinking about our talk last night," he said, without looking at me.

"What about it?" I asked. He dropped his hood and looked at me.

"We—I—will not live forever, and there is so much more that I need to teach you. This world we live in has much more in it than you could imagine, and you've only seen a sliver of it. We aren't the only special people in it."

"I know," I replied.

"Looking at the Emperor and all of his immortality has taught me that much." Ember shook his head and turned away from me. "No, there are others. Others with gifts who can do things that even a Warper would envy." My brow rose. I hadn't expected this, but I had only known about Warpers for a couple of years. The list of things I didn't know was likely long. I trusted Ember, though, and if he was telling me this, then eventually he would show me.

He went silent for a moment. Was he thinking, or simply looking at the city? I moved to stand in front of him, but he spun around to face me before I could.

"We have a job," he said. I began to protest, but he raised his hand.

"Let me finish. After this job, that's it for me. I will not be taking contracts for the most part. Only here and there, to preserve my ability to warp."

Certainly he wasn't serious, I thought to myself as he continued.

"I will train you, and only approve your contracts after going over it with you."

"Wait, what?" I couldn't believe what I was hearing. Ember couldn't just up and stop doing this. He had always told me that this is simply what we did. And as horrific as it sounded, Ember was good at what he did. What we did.

I looked around at the city as I searched for a proper response, and nearby I saw a man with a bicycle. It jolted a question into my head that escaped my lips instantly.

"What about living?" I asked.

Ember turned his head slightly. "Living?"

"Yeah. I'm sure you don't have some massive pile of yolars saved up. How will you live? How will you support yourself?"

He paused and rubbed his beard. "I could always just live off of your earnings," he said casually.

"It was a serious question, you know," I said.

"I know. I've been a Warper for over thirty years. Many people know my name, a few even know my face, and all know what I have done, and can do. After all that, all I really have are my weapons, a few homes, and a hound with a weak bladder. I didn't go much in the way of saving. Never thought I'd make it this long, to tell the truth."

What was happening? As we stood on this building in the sunlight and snow drifted down around us, I was beginning to see a version of Ember that, in these two years, I hadn't seen. He was, under it all, just a man. I'd always known it, but I'd always seen him as more.

"This job," he continued, "is going to be a big one. I haven't got all the details yet, but if we do it—and yes, I mean *we*—then living shouldn't be an issue."

I was speechless. Standing there under my cloak like a pile of caprong droppings. This must be some contract.

"Just to make sure we are clear, this is *my* contract," Ember said. "My blade, my kill, my earnings. You will come along to observe and do what I tell you. Do you understand?"

It was back to business as usual. Stern and menacing.

"I understand."

He put his cloak hood up and leaned in towards me and looked me in the eye.

"This issue you have with killing." I swallowed as my throat went dry. "It ends now. You bury it deep down and never look at it again. I have been giving you a cut for helping, but that stops now."

My eyes widened. My surprise was replaced by sudden anger.

"You know my family needs this. I'm all they have," I said, in almost a growl.

Ember straightened up. "I do know. Shorn and the twins are the closest things to real friends or family that I have had in years. I know how much you love them, and that's why I'm doing this. If you want them to eat, to live, then be the man you want to be and provide. Earn it for them. You love what you are, but hate what you have to do. What you were born to do. Well, tired is the arm that swings the blade, and it's a burden you must live with."

He turned from me so fast that his cloak rose from the ground.

"It may not be now; it may not even be a contract. But you will kill, and you will do it not because I say so, but because of them. So that they can live. So that you can live."

I felt like I was glaring a hole in his back as he spoke. I could feel my nostrils flaring and my breath felt like a pack of people running. I hated him for a moment. I hated what he had said and the decision he had made, while, at the same time, I knew it was final. There was no point in feeling this way, but I couldn't help it.

"Come; we have to get going. Our contact is waiting at The Clarkton for us," he said as he turned to glance at me. His eyes widened a little. "Take that anger and save it for when you need it, Lox. Use it for later, but for now, put it away. The Clarkton. Now."

He turned and warped away.

Fuming inside, I had no choice but to follow. My curiosity had taken hold long before our conversation faded. Angry as I was, I wanted to know what the contract was. It must have been big for such a large pay out. It was likely dangerous, too. For now, I did as I was told. My anger would have to be put away for the moment. I checked my belt to make sure everything was there, and I warped off the roof to the furthest one away that I could see. The Clarkton was on the far side of Thera, and the journey there would take some effort.

Warping was funny that way. In a battle we could warp with almost no drawbacks, because it was a small distance. A couple feet here and there was fine. Even long distances didn't bother us much. It was the continuous large warps, though, that became a problem. The further the warp, the more it pulled the body. The longer we were gone to wherever it is we go when we warp away, the weaker we are when we reappear.

Ember held up to this strain better than me. The decades of practice had made his body stronger. But for me, this trip was going to require some food after. After the bread last night, I normally wouldn't eat for another day or so, but if I didn't replenish after this long warp, I'd be asleep for half a day in no time.

I warped and warped again, clearing large spans of the city. It was just my luck that Thera was the largest city in all the five kingdoms. Had this been Walden or Pradeep I would have made the trip and cleared most of the kingdom already. This entire time, I hadn't caught glimpse of Ember. His eyes weren't as young as mine, so he couldn't see further away, and as a result he couldn't really warp a larger distance. What he was, though, was fast. He was able to recover quicker and rapidly warp with almost no rest in between.

I warped to another building and stopped to catch my breath. I had to lean over and place my hands on my knees just to keep from fall down, because I was feeling dizzy. After a couple of minutes, I warped to the street below, and I slowly walked in the direction of my destination. Thankfully it was close. I knew where The Clarkton was; I just had never been to it. To be honest, I had never even been in this part of Thera at all. None of the previous contracts had required us to travel this far out.

All of Thera was nice. One of the best places to live in the Prime Sovereignty. This area, however, was depressing. Even more depressing than where my home was. I knew it wasn't as nice as the area surrounding the Main Statue—no area was—but this was downright bad. The homes were smaller and built more out of wood and mud than stones or steel. I hadn't seen a carriage for miles, and if a bicycle ventured into this part of town, the rider would likely be killed for it.

The most disturbing part was that a lot of people were just living on the streets. Dressed in clothes stained in a mixture of blood and dirt, people begged others who were likely as poor as them for yolars.

This part of Thera was dangerously close to Kameace, and it showed. The kingdom of Kameace was by far the most poverty-ridden portion of the Prime Sovereignty and some of its traits had trickled up into Thera. I didn't want to cause a panic when I warped to the street, so I selected a less crowded part. If a person saw me appear, they would likely assume I was there to kill somebody, and that wouldn't go well. I kept to the walls and shadows as much as I could, and began walking towards The Clarkton.

"Boy, boy," a voice called to me—a woman sitting on the ground, wrapped in a blanket that was covered with dirt and yellow stains that I assumed were urine. Her voice was raspy and crackled as she spoke. She coughed into her hand several times before turning away to spit on the ground. She looked back up to me. Her hair was thin as strings and was gray with what appeared to be dirt. The skin on her face was waxy, and the lines under her eyes made it look like she hadn't slept in years. She stood, stumbled some, and then approached me.

Purely on instinct my hand twitched towards my blade. When I realized what I had done, I felt ashamed.

"Please, boy, I haven't ate in eight days." She wasn't close to me, but when she spoke I could smell her breath and was instantly reminded of the bag that had been placed on my head while confronting Ashland. I pulled out a silver yolar. In an instant I realized it was a mistake.

Her lips parted with a wide smile as she saw the round silver yolar. Her teeth, the ones she had, anyway, were darker than her hair. She reached for it, and was suddenly pushed out of the way and down to the ground by another. This man was as dirty as she was—maybe even more. He was bare chested and had on only trousers, and I could see his ribs with ease. The snow falling on his bare upper body was a vivid contrast to his dirty skin. Luckily, it wasn't cold out, and the snow never stuck to the ground, because this man was also barefoot. He snatched the coin from my hand, and this time I did grab my dagger. I only intended to scare him, but before I could, the woman was up and on her feet.

"It's mine, Emo, you dirty pile of lopeseal!" the older woman screamed as she jumped and clawed at his bare chest. The man, Emo, was clearly as surprised as I was, and was on his back in seconds as she continued to attack him. Several other people emerged, all as dirty and smelly as the first two, and joined in the fight. I hadn't intended to start all of this. I made a mental note to keep my yolar bag close and hidden while in this part of Thera.

I turned to walk away from the scene and almost walked directly into a small child.

"Sorry. I didn't see you," I said as I looked down at him. Or her. It was hard to tell. The child had long dark hair like a girl, but under the dirt and smudges on its face were boyish features. The child, too, was barefoot, and wore a pair of brown trousers and a shirt that was two or three sizes too big. The child said nothing as it looked up at me and stretched out its hand. I thought about simply stepping aside and going on my way; then I heard a grunt and scream again from the fighting happening behind me. This wasn't a place for a child.

I dropped to one knee and pulled out another silver yolar. I didn't have many left on me but I did have some stashed away at Ember's place. I held the yolar up to the sun a little and twirled it. The child winced as the sunlight bounced and hit him, or her, in the eye. It simply looked at me.

"Do you know what this is?" I asked. He, or she, shook its head and a smiled stretched on its face. Despite the dirty appearance, the child's teeth were oddly white. I narrowed my eyes at the child. That was curious.

"Take this, keep it close, and run along."

The child opened its eyes wide and slowly removed the currency from my hand, placing it inside a pocket of its trousers.

"Get some food, and some clean clothes. That should be plenty." I glanced over my shoulder at the others still fighting. One man was stretched out unconscious now. "Run along now," I said as I turned to face the child. My brow rose some as I found an empty space before me. The child had gone. At least it was smart enough to listen to me.

6

Ember was sitting on a wooden bench waiting for me when I finally made my way to The Clarkton. There was another wooden bench to the left of him that had a rather large man sleeping on it. He easily weighed more than a couple hundred pounds and was wearing some sort of red outfit.

"Slow, as usual," Ember said. I didn't answer him immediately, because I couldn't stop looking at this large man in red. I imagined that getting through doors would be hard for a man his size.

"I had to walk the last part of the trip, and I'm starving now," I replied as I moved to sit down beside him. The bench wasn't as sturdy as the one that held the sleeping man; it wobbled and gave a little as I put my weight down.

"I remember the days when I couldn't warp across Thera," Ember said. "It gets easier in time. Come on, you can eat inside."

He stood from the bench.

"I just sat down," I said. I had made this entire trip, and now I wanted a moment, just a few seconds to breath. I actually felt nauseous. Nauseous and hungry, and those were two horrible feelings to have together.

Ember removed his hood. "Keeper as my witness, if you don't get—" I cut him off mid-threat and stood up from the bench. He pushed the door open, and I followed him in.

The Clarkton, from the outside, appeared to be composed of mud and stone, like most buildings in this part of Thera. Inside, however, it was something else. I stood inside the door, simply looking at the marvel before me. The inner structure walls were steel. Strong, sturdy, and likely expensive to build. A quality building hidden in the open, disguised.

While the building of The Clarkton was disguised as less-than-savory, its clients *were* actually less-than-savory. From what I knew of the place, The Clarkton was one of a kind. No other place like it existed in any of the kingdoms. The Clarkton was a not only a place where you could eat, sleep, drink and smoke, it was also neutral ground. No matter what your background outside the walls, once inside, everybody was equal. There wasn't any violence allowed. Those were the rules.

A palace guard could share a drink with a wanted murderer inside, and neither would fear or attack the other. Even though it was early, The Clarkton had many people inside.

At the bar was a group of men, all larger. They were all dressed in black and having drinks. Judging from the club-like weapons that rested beside them, they were likely guards from Kameace. The guards there were known to enjoy bashing skulls in with clubs. It didn't have the elegance of a sword, or the precision of a spear, but it got the job done.

The various tables spread out everywhere seated everyone from the homeless to fallen nobility. The fallen nobility didn't even enjoy The Clarkton, but, for one crime or another, they couldn't get service anywhere else.

"Try not to look so shocked, boy," Ember whispered into my ear. I hadn't realized I had frozen so much. Ember walked past me. "It's just a bar," he said over his shoulder as he pulled a chair from a table.

"Ember! Keeper strike me down. Is that you?"

A man from behind the bar had called out. He was a short, wide, and round man. He made me think of Sprits just by sight. He had long brown hair, and his forehead appeared larger than normal due to his receding hairline. As he shouted Ember's name, many of the people in the bar looked in our direction.

Some raised their brows as they looked on, while others froze instantly at mention of the name. Talk about awkward. It was unnerving having so many eyes on us at once. Even for that brief moment.

Well, it was unnerving for me. Ember didn't even seem to notice. He just stood beside his chair.

"Friend of yours?" I asked. He said nothing. I looked back to the round man and felt a hitch in my breath at what happened next.

He warped.

From behind the bar to in front of us, in a second. When he appeared in front of us, his large belly jiggled and he was breathing hard. Warping could make a person tired, but simply warping a few feet shouldn't. I found this amusing and saddening at the same time. He was breathing harder than me, and I had just crossed the largest kingdom in the Prime Sovereignty.

Ember cleared his throat and eyed me. I had seen that look on his face before. He did not like this man, and people Ember didn't like usually didn't live long. But like him or not, this man was clearly fond of Ember.

"I thought I was seeing a ghost. How long has it been? Five, six years?" The man hugged Ember and then placed a hand on his shoulder. I could see Ember's lip twitch slightly. Clearly the no-violence rules of The Clarkton were keeping him in line, but his level of discomfort was evident, and I did all I could to hold in my laughter.

"Seven, actually," Ember said as he forcefully threw the man's hand from his shoulder.

"Seven? Time goes by too fast when you're traveling the Kingdoms." The man stopped talking and looked at me. "Who's your friend?"

"He's not my friend," Ember said gruffly. I looked at him with my face crumpled and brow raised. He caught my eye. "He's my pupil. Lox Norcros, meet Turk Clarkton the Fifth." He exhaled as he made the introduction, as if doing it against his will. "Owner of this fine establishment. A man known to do anything, if enough yolars are involved, and a retired Warper who manages to retain his powers through deeds unknown."

"His pupil? Pupil!" Turk said loudly as he looked at me and shook my hand. "Three Warpers in one place? That's like a night when it's not raining. It's unheard of. Keeper, what a day." He began walking to the bar and waved us over. "Come on, you two, here with me at the bar."

He leaned in and spoke to the guards from Kameace, who looked at me and Ember as we approached, and then got up from their seats and found a table to use instead.

"So, what brings you in? Food? Drink? Smoke?" Turk asked as he leaned on the bar and grinned at us. "I can even offer you a companion for the night." He looked at me with a wink as I removed my hood.

"Turk, why would we come here for drink or smoke? We don't have yolars to waste, and we aren't looking for women," Ember said as he looked around the bar.

He was half truthful, and not just about the women. To purchase drink, or smoke, would be pointless for Warpers. For some reason or another, internal poisons have no effect on us. Unlike normal men, Ember, Turk, and I could drink our weight in wine, and smoke for a day, but it wouldn't affect us at all.

This was another of the many things that even older Warpers couldn't explain. It was odd, because we couldn't get drunk, and even if a poison arrow hit us, it would have no effect. Our bodies were simply immune. Despite that, we could still get sick naturally, and could even succumb to that sickness if it was strong enough. What was even more odd was that Ember was a fan of drinking, and there weren't many things he liked more than wine. He said he simply liked the taste. He must have really hated this Turk, to turn down wine.

"Give the boy some food," Ember said as he pulled out his yolar bag slowly.

"Keep it," Turk said as he walked to the end of the bar, removing a plate of bread and meat from another patron and setting it down in front of me.

"Eat up, Liam."

"It's Lox," I said as I picked up the bread.

"Of course it is," Turk said, without even looking at me.

"Turk, I'm here looking for somebody," Ember said as he continued to peer around the bar. Turk rubbed his hands together. "Calm down, Turk, I just said we aren't here for women."

As they continued to speak, I continued to eat. This bread was good. I tried the meat. It was even better than the bread.

"This is really good," I said; my cheeks felt like they were about to explode. Turk beamed at me.

"You like that, huh? All of our stuff is imported from across the Pradeep border. Eat up, kid, you'll need your strength."

This made me slow down chewing. Why would I need my strength? He stammered some after he said that. Like he didn't mean for it to slip when it did.

"For the trip back, I mean," he said as he quickly turned back to Ember.

"So you're here for a job? You know the rules."

Ember waved his hand. "No, I'm meeting a contact here."

Turk nodded.

"I'll leave you two to it then."

Just like that, he walked away and into a back room. This seemed strange to me, but Ember seemed happy to see Turk leave. He stuck his hand on my plate and took my last chunk of meat, and tossed it in his mouth. "Keeper, this is good," he said as he licked his fingers and looked down on my plate.

I knew it was good. I also knew I had intended to eat that last piece myself. I pushed the plate away.

"What is a lopeseal?" I asked him.

"Trust me, you don't want to know," he said grimly.

"Why?"

I was interrupted before I could even finish.

"Mr. Ember," a voice came from behind us.

We turned around and saw a thin, well-dressed man standing in front of us. We were sitting down, and he was standing up, yet we all seemed the same height. He must have been rather short. He was clearly older than me, but not by much. His eyes were thin; his hair was jet black and lank and fell just behind his ears. His upper lip and chin were covered by the same grade of hair, and he wore a small pendant around his neck.

"Who's asking?" Ember said sharply as his hand disappeared under his cloak.

"Are you Mr. Ember?" the man asked again. This time his voice was different. It was pure. It was alluring. I felt like I could listen to him talk forever.

"Yes. I am Ember," Ember responded. For a moment I was surprised, but then, who couldn't respond to a voice like that?

The man turned and looked at me. "And just who are you?"

"Lox," I said immediately. The word flew out of my mouth before I even wanted it too.

"Lox," the man said as he stepped closer to me. "Are you a Warper as well? Did Ember tell the barman the truth when he said that?"

I wanted to ask him why he was asking all these questions. I didn't even want to answer, but that voice was sunlight piercing through darkness, and the more he spoke the more the sunlight washed over me. "Yes, I am."

"Good," the man said as he clapped his hands. Everything suddenly returned to normal. No more sunshine. No more alluring tone that I could listen to forever. What was going on, and who was this guy? He was beginning to give me an uneasy feeling.

"I'm Jolin, your contact." He shook my hand first and then went to shake Ember's. When he tried to pull his hand away from Ember's, however, Ember didn't let go. If anything, he continued to grip it tighter.

"Mr. Ember?" the man said as he looked at his hand with his eyes wide. Ember pulled him in close.

"I know what you are. It's been a long time since I felt the power of a Tongue wash over me, but it's a feeling I'd never forget. Do it again, and—"

"Let's not be hasty, Mr. Ember. Remember that we are all on the same side." He jerked his hand back.

Had Ember called this Jolin a Tongue? What was a Tongue?

"I wasn't aware that you were bringing another, Mr. Ember," Jolin said as he rubbed his hand.

"He's my pupil. He comes, or I don't."

I looked from Ember to Jolin, who was acting as if Ember's menacing tone wasn't bothering him at all.

"No need to be that way, Mr. Ember. Surely two Warpers are better than one. Keeper knows the odds aren't in our favor on this job. So our employer should be fine with that."

Our employer? So this Jolin person wasn't in charge, yet he knew about the job. He wasn't a Warper, but he knew about the contract. This was becoming more and more confusing. Before I could voice my thoughts to Ember, he glanced around the room.

Whatever was going on, he noticed it before me. I could see some people leaving, while people who once had weapons at their side were suddenly holding them now, and looking at us. Most of them looked like they had been in a few good fights before, mainly those four guards from Kameace.

"Turk, I'm going to kill you," Ember said through snarling teeth.

Jolin slowly backed away as the people in the room holding weapons began to stand up and face us.

"Yes. Mr. Turk allowed our employer to break the rules of The Clarkton just this once."

"He was paid well, I assume," Ember said as he removed his dagger. I followed his actions and drew my dagger as well.

"Oh, I'm sure. I'm a part of the team, just like you, Mr. Ember. I don't get all the details. I was just sent here to escort you back, assuming you pass this little test our employer wanted."

"Test?" I said, finally finding words. Jolin looked at me and nodded.

"Yes. Our employer wanted to make sure Mr. Ember is as good as his legend suggests he is. The entire Prime Sovereignty will feel the effects of this job, so we have to make sure we have the best. Apparently, that includes you now, too, Mr. Lox. As you've gathered, these people have been paid to try and kill you. Paid nicely, I would believe. If you survive, then meet me outside by the carriage. If you don't, then—" He paused for a moment, exhaled, and then turned and walked away.

Two women, who looked like twins and held small knives, parted and allowed Jolin to exit before locking the door behind him. Ember looked at me.

"Now we know why Turk said you'd need your energy. Take your cloak off, and get ready."

We both removed our cloaks at the same time. With this many people attacking, the cloaks could get in the way. Our greaves and bracers were all we had as protection.

"Now would be a good time to get over that not-killing idea," Ember said to me.

"You may be right," I responded, but in my head I was already thinking of ways to put them down without killing them. I took a deep breath, tightened my grip on my dagger, grabbed one of my throwing knives, and warped into the crowd of waiting killers.

7

As soon as I reappeared, I felt a hard blow to my back. It was as if my spine was going to explode through the front of my body. I stumbled into a table, and in the time it took me to focus, I realized I was surrounded. The two female twins holding daggers had targeted me first.

They were identical in every way. Both had sharp noses, thin lips, high cheeks, and black hair that was in locks. The daggers they brandished were identical, also. Steel that was almost a foot long, with a black handle that had a red stone embedded into the base. Even though they wanted to kill me, I had to admit that they had some finely crafted weapons.

These twin attackers were joined by a very pale-skinned man. He stood almost seven feet tall, had arms like tree trunks and a chest that a statue would envy. He had a long ponytail, but was otherwise bald. Oddly, he didn't have a weapon, but with arms like that, I was sure he could get the job done. He seemed more mountain than man. As I looked at him, I was ashamed at the fear I felt. I had never seen a person this large, and outside of Ember, I had never seen a man so scary.

They came in closer around me and advanced. I glanced down and warped. In a few seconds I appeared again in the exact same spot. My ruse had worked. The three of them had assumed I would appear in another area of The Clarkton, and were looking away from me. I didn't hesitate. I went for the twins first—they seemed to be the weaker of the trio.

First the female twin on the left. I moved in by doing a roll and emerged with a slash to the back of her left knee. I had seen Ember perform this move often, and it was very effective. Naturally she swung in reaction, but I warped quickly to her other side, and proceed to kick her right knee. The sound of bone breaking echoed even over all the chaos. She dropped her dagger instantly and fell, grabbing at her knee.

As she dropped down, I delivered a solid blow with my fist to her chin that sent her rolling to the ground. All of this took maybe twenty seconds, and now I was down one attacker for the moment. This minor achievement seemed pointless, seeing as we still had a room full of people trying to murder us.

The moment of surprise I had had over them was over, as her sister and the man mountain advanced on me.

"No," the man mountain said in a voice like thunder as he used both of his massive forearms and attacked the woman in front of him. "Him mine," he bellowed as he repeatedly bashed on the fallen woman in front of him, causing blood to cover the floor. Even though she had intended to kill me, I still pitied the way she died. Pummeled to death by a being that was more a giant than he was a man.

He stood tall and proud with a smile on his face as blood dripped from his forearms. He advanced on me, crossing several feet with every step. He, much like the homeless outside, had on no shoes. In rapid succession I hurled a throwing knife at each foot, hoping to slow him down. I had no such luck, because the knives bounced off of his bare feet as if they were made of iron. What was this guy? I warped across the bar.

He was too strong to fight head on, and I would need

Ember to help with him. Ember had issues of his own—he was fighting a group of four people at once. There were several others, trying to advance in on him as well, but the four fighting him had created a circle so close that other attackers had trouble getting close. Many people seemed to pay him more attention than me, which I could use to my advantage.

I warped onto the bar of The Clarkton so that I could get a good view of Ember's circle, stepping on plates and mugs as I appeared. The circle surrounding him was tight, but I could do it. A few attackers saw me appear on the bar and headed my way. They seemed to be workers of some sort. They all had on dirty clothes similar to those worn by the people who worked in the mines, and had tools for weapons.

They were likely just trying to make some extra money, and I didn't want to kill them. That aside, they were still trying to make extra money by killing me. They were not professionals and posed little threat to me or Ember. They could wait.

I focused on Ember's circle of attackers. Warping in too close could put me in the line of his fight, so I warped just close enough for some to see me. As I had hoped, many of them had finally seen that I was a Warper too, and some of the crowd shifted to me, joining the mine workers who had rushed me. It seemed like a good plan—until a massive club from a Kameace guard swung and almost took my upper body off.

It was so close that I didn't even have time to warp; I simply jumped out of the way. While the club missed me, it did connect with some of my would-be attackers. Mainly the men dressed like mine workers. They fell quickly and didn't stand up again.

Clubs were big and strong, but if you took the chance and allowed your prey to get in close enough, they became almost useless. Seeing as how he was used to a club, I was willing to bet that he wasn't good at hand-to-hand.

Dagger in hand, I ran in as close as I could, warping quickly and then reappearing directly where I had left again. I figured it had worked once—why not again? I was wrong. This guard was so dumb that he hadn't even looked around for me. Instead he was looking at the spot where I left, and was all but scratching his head in confusion. My reappearance caused his head to jerk back in surprise.

I used my dagger at this moment and stabbed him in his arm. He grunted and then punched my shoulder.

Badly aimed attack or not, it still hurt. He went to punch again and, with few options left, I absorbed the punch again by placing my shoulder in front of it. Quickly I grabbed his extended arm and let my dagger attack once, twice, three times. Each time at target points of his arm. He screamed this time as his arm fell limp at his side. Those wounds wouldn't kill him, but it would make using that arm painful and difficult.

I dodged another attack from behind me, and delivered a swift kick to the attacker's stomach. It was one of the mine workers again, who had managed to get back up. I didn't focus much on him. The kick had did its job, and he was sprawled on the ground again.

The Kameace guard screamed in fury as he pulled his club back and tried to attack. I eyed the area of the fallen twin, then warped to her and grabbed her dagger. In seconds I was back in front of my club-wielding attacker and stabbed him in the foot. He fell back so hard that his head hit the ground. He lay there, bleeding and unmoving. I hoped he would be out of the way long enough for us to handle the rest.

I warped again. I wanted to thin the herd, and to do so I would have to move around. I couldn't stand my ground as much as Ember, who currently had more than seven bodies on the floor near him. Free from the no-violence rule, he was making quick work of the attackers. Ember couldn't take all of the credit, though. The man mountain seemed to be killing as many of the attackers as Ember was. Lucky us.

Warping, I appeared near a short man who was trying to advance through the crowd that surrounded Ember. He saw me and swung his sword.

This man was short, but his sword was unnervingly large. His face twisted and his stout features shined with sweat. I was too slow on the dodge and his sword clipped me on the leg. Pain flooded my body as I stumbled and fell through a table. I had never been injured in a fight before. In my mind I knew it was only a cut, but it was deep. Deep enough that standing, while possible, wouldn't be easy. The short man removed his helmet, showing off curled blond hair as he kicked chairs out of the way to get to me. I had no throwing knives left, but I had fallen near the twin whose knee I had attacked. I reached for her dagger.

The man was getting closer as I stretched my arm, trying to grab the dagger. He got to me before I got to the knife, and he raised the massive sword and swung down. I rolled to the side as where I had been seconds ago was shattered by the falling blade. The sword sliced through the table I'd fallen on with ease, and became lodged in the floor. The man struggled to get the sword free. I let the twin's dagger fly, and it found its mark in the man's eye.

My heart almost stopped. I hadn't been aiming for his eye. I had been aiming for his shoulder. That would have slowed him down enough for me to attack.

Instantly he fell back and put his hand to his eye to grab the blade. I felt a touch of relief that he wasn't dead. I wanted to retrieve the knife so I could keep it. It really was a well-crafted dagger.

Its removal could aid in his recovery, and that I didn't want. Many of the attackers were dead, and spread through the bar now. It seemed that Ember, too, had begun to move around instead of standing still inside of the circle of attackers. There was only one person left, and he was currently hitting Ember in the stomach. Hard.

The man mountain from earlier. He was, of course, all that was left. Ember attacked the hand holding him, and then warped to the man's side and went for his stomach with the dagger. I'm sure he would have preferred to attack the neck, but the man was too tall.

Ember's dagger connected with the man mountains stomach, but didn't seem to affect his thick skin. Instead he snarled and hit Ember with a backhanded blow that sent him to the ground. He landed on the dead bodies of the Kameace guards. My attacker still screamed on the ground as he tried to remove the dagger from his eye.

I spun around and reached for his sword. It was lodged in the ground still and it took a few kicks before it came free. These kicks alone, because of my cut leg, inflicted more pain on me than the entire fight had.

Sword in hand, I warped closer to the area where Ember and the man mountain were.

Ember had advanced towards the bar, but was in no way winning in this fight. The man before him stood and blocked as Ember delivered timed and precise blows to areas known to weaken an attacker. This man, however, shrugged them off and continued in, grabbing Ember by the neck and slamming him on the bar. I acted as fast as I could.

Sword in hand, I warped on top of the bar once more.

The man mountain seemed to have forgotten about me as he looked up and his long ponytail swished. He tilted his head slightly. I could barely breathe. I knew what I needed to do, and hated that I had to do it, but he was killing Ember.

I had to kill this man mountain.

I swung the sword back and, with all the power I had left, I let the blade fall and connect with the man's neck.

There was a loud thud as if I had just struck a tree.

"How?" I said out loud. The sword hadn't even left a scratch on the man.

He looked at me and smiled. "Clipasie don't hurt. Clipasie strong," The man grunted at me. Ember had his blade in hand again. The man mountain was focused on me, but still had Ember on the bar by the neck.

He took one of his massive hands off of Ember's neck and grabbed me by my cut leg and threw me to the ground like I was a child's toy.

In that instant, Ember drove his dagger through the bottom of the man's chin. It made a sticky sound as the blade disappeared into the man's skull. He fell down on the bar as his grip on Ember faded away.

Ember coughed, rubbing his neck and extending his hand to me to help me up.

"Clipasie. Freakishly strong and almost invulnerable due to their thick skin," Ember said as he looked around. "Nobody is sure where they come from, though. Never seen one so short, either. And I definitely have never seen one in Thera."

Ember tilted his head back and point under his chin. "They have a small spot of soft tissue right under here. Keeper knows it's hard to get to, but if you can, you can kill them"

"I'll keep that in mind," I said as I slid down to the floor and began to inspect my leg.

Ember passed me a portion of cloth to wrap it with. "Just keep it tight, it's not that bad."

Our heads both jerked towards the wall when we heard a noise come from behind it. I tried to stand, but Ember placed a firm hand on my shoulder and shook his head. His eyes narrowed for a second, and then in the next they grew wide and seemed to be set on fire.

His calm tone shifted as he began to breathe heavy and his jaw clenched.

"What?" I said as he picked up the sword I had used to try and kill the Clipasie.

He didn't even look down on me as he spoke through gritted teeth.

"Turk," he said, as he hefted the sword and walked towards the back room.

8

I sat on the floor. It was hard, trying to deal with the pain, while at the same time forcing myself to look away from the blood-stained cloth wrapped around my leg. A few minutes went by before Ember reemerged from the back room. I heard no screams, and I heard no shouts. Yet he had that look in his eye. The same look I had seen many times after he had completed a contract. A faint smile would dance on his lips, and for a moment Ember experienced satisfaction. I also noticed that his sword had been cleaner when he entered the room, and now it was rather bloody.

"Turk?" I asked as I began to get up slowly. Ember put on his cloak, grabbed mine and then helped me up.

"The Clarkton will be needing a new owner, that's for sure."

I shook my head as he placed my arm around his neck to help me walk.

I didn't respond. Turk had set us up. He may not have known about me being with Ember, but it hadn't stopped him either way. And he and Ember had been friends, supposedly, yet he still was okay with possibly getting him killed. Then, in the back of my head, I thought, what if Turk had such faith in Ember's ability to survive that he had known he would be okay? I shook the thoughts from my head. It was still a horrible thing to do. Then why did I feel bad for him? I pushed the remaining thoughts of concern out of my mind. He was dead, and I had myself to worry about.

We finally made it to the door and, with my weight leaning on him, Ember kicked it open and we shuffled through. As we stepped outside, I could see the young man Jolin standing beside a very nice carriage. It was larger than normal, able to easily fit six people. Maybe even more. The carriage was covered with a red coat of paint, was outlined in gold trim, and, from what I could see, was being pulled by four solid white caprongs, with a driver at the ready. Whoever our employer was, they clearly were very wealthy.

I looked around us. Having such a nice carriage in this part of Thera was sure to attract attention. Or so I thought. No matter the direction I looked, the street seemed to be empty. What had gone on out here? Before, the street had been absolutely alive with people; now it was deserted.

"Mr. Ember, Mr. Lox," Jolin said as he clapped. "I'm happy to see you two made it out. I feel better doing this job with you two on my side." He opened the carriage door for us. Ember only looked at him.

Jolin brushed some snowflakes from his hair.

"Mr. Ember, I assure you, I am not your enemy. Our first meeting wasn't ideal, but we all have a part to play. I have some things on the inside that can help Mr. Lox. He seems in a bad way," Jolin said as he looked at my leg.

"I'm fine," I replied. Naturally, I was lying. My leg hurt like you wouldn't believe, and standing on it was only making it worse.

"Come on," Ember said as he helped me inside the carriage.

This carriage was nicer on the inside than the outside. In seventeen years of living, I had never been inside a carriage, so I had nothing to compare it to, but I was pretty sure this was a high end one.

The seats were made out of some sort of soft material that had a slight sheen to it. Large windows were on both sides of the carriage, and there was even a miniature ice box on the inside which was intended for food and drink.

"This is pretty awesome," I said out loud as I touched the fabric again with my fingertips. This carriage was nicer than my home.

"Shut up and move over," Ember said as he tried to get inside the carriage. I positioned myself inside, close to the window facing The Clarkton.

It had once been intended as a safe zone for all who entered its doors, but now there was so much death on the inside. Ember had left so many bodies. I wasn't sure what would become of it now, but I doubted it would be the same after all the bloodshed.

Surprisingly, sitting there still on the bench was the large man in red from before. He wasn't lying down anymore, but it was still him. I felt as if he was looking directly at me. His eyes seemed unnaturally dark brown, and for a moment I felt that I had seen him before. He waved at the carriage, very slowly, as if he was cautious of the interaction with us, even though he was a couple feet away. He smiled for a brief moment, and flashed a set of white teeth.

Very white teeth. Why had I—

"Mr. Lox," Jolin said as he removed his jacket and rolled up his sleeves.

"Yeah?" I said. The carriage began moving.

"I need your leg." He opened a small box. Inside were various vials filled with a assorted liquids of different colors, bandages, small knives, needles, string and syringes. I adjusted myself and began removing the bloody bandage from my leg. The cut was worse than I had thought.

"He got you good, didn't he?" Ember said as he eyed the wound.

My leg stung and throbbed as we finished removing the cloth, which was so full of blood that it dripped as we discarded it in a small pan. Jolin reached for some of the vials in his box. His arms were both exposed, and his left arm had black tattoos on it that ran up to his shoulder.

"You from Galcon?" Ember asked as he saw the tattoos. He himself had similar tattoos, as did most of the men born and raised in Galcon.

Jolin shook his head from side to side as he examined my leg. "I was only raised in Galcon. I was born here in Thera." The carriage jerked some and made us bounce inside, which caused me to wince. Jolin took a deep breath and said, "This may hurt a little bit," and poured a small vial of blue liquid on my wound.

I thought my leg had hurt before, but whatever was in this vial was like liquid lighting. My leg was on fire, burning to the core. I felt as if my bone itself was about to explode. I clinched at the soft, cushioned seats of the carriage as my eyes watered, and then, just like that, every ounce of pain faded away like melting snow. No pain, no nothing. I couldn't even feel my leg anymore. I glanced down to make sure my leg was still attached. Even as I looked at it and moved it, I couldn't feel it.

"What is this stuff?" I asked Jolin.

"Something for the pain," he replied, pulling out the threaded needle and beginning to close the wound. "Just try to stay calm."

I watched him weave in and out between my parted flesh. It was odd watching him do this, yet feeling absolutely no pain. Whatever it was that he had poured from the vial would have been great to have had as a child. I hurt myself pretty often as a kid. My fascination with knives had started early.

Jolin stop working and reached into his box once more, removing a vial that looked a lot like blood. "Drink this," he said as he passed me the vial.

I looked at it and then glanced at Ember. He eyed me, shrugged, and then returned his gaze to Jolin. "What is it?" I said as I took the vial to look at it.

"Well, you know it's not poison," Jolin said. "Poison doesn't work on Warpers." He had a point there. It couldn't kill me. "Still don't trust me?" he asked. It was the way he asked. I heard his voice again as if it was the first time. It made things stand still. I couldn't feel the carriage move, I couldn't hear anything but his voice. That voice set my soul on fire, and I couldn't help but answer.

"I don't trust you," I blurted out. "You left us in there just to see what would happen, and I'm like this because of you."

He opened his mouth to speak again, but before he could get the words out, Ember drew his dagger and threw it at Jolin. The blade passed just by Jolin's face, and stuck into the back part of the carriage. Jolin froze as he held the his tools in one hand. A small drop of blood appeared on his face.

Jolin cleared his throat, using the back of his hand and wiped the blood away. "Mr. Ember, may I ask why you did that?" he said as his voice rose a little. Ember stood in a slumped position and removed his blade.

"Don't do that. Not to me, and not to Lox. Do you understand me? I won't tell you again."

"Very well," Jolin said as he returned to working on my leg.

"Do what?" I said as I looked at Ember.

He put his blade away. "Jolin here is what we call a Tongue."

"I personally hate that term. It's offensive," Jolin said, without looking away from my leg.

"A Tongue?" I asked.

Jolin let out a deep breath, but didn't stop working on my leg. "Tongues are people, able to use the tones of their voice to put a person in a—" He thought for a moment. "Euphoric state. Once in these states, a person must always tell us the truth. Even if they don't want to. I'm sure you have noticed a funny feeling consume you when I ask certain questions. Well, now you know why."

Jolin glared at Ember and stuck my leg. *Funny feeling?* I thought to myself. Is that how he thought it felt? It was more than funny. It was enjoyable.

"What he's leaving out is that tongues, rare as they may be, always find themselves working as spies or secret collectors for higher authority. A Tongue, with years of secrets, can take a Kingdom down as efficiently as any blade can."

"We have a long trip ahead of us. Can we just ride in silence until we get to Pradeep, please?" Jolin asked as he looked from me to Ember. His tone seemed to have changed. Before he had been upbeat, fun, and seemingly confident; now he seemed isolated. Was he ashamed of what he was? In comparison to a person destined to kill, it didn't seem so bad.

Ember said nothing as he slouched back and relaxed in the carriage chair.

"What's in Pradeep?" I asked.

"Not what, but who," Jolin replied. "Our employer. The person who has hired me, you, Mr. Ember, and the other members of our team. I encourage you to drink that—the numbing agent will be wearing off before I can finish closing your wound. That will put you into a deep sleep until it's over."

I considered my options. As if I had many. And then felt a tingle in my leg. The feeling was slowly coming back, and so was the pain. Jolin stuck my leg with the needle, and this time I winced. Quickly, I uncorked the vial and downed the blood-like liquid. It tasted horrible. Like a mixture of dirt and metal that went down slow and stuck to my teeth in the process.

"Relax. Allow it to work," Jolin said. I gave him the empty vial back and leaned back in my chair. Ember was still awake; he wasn't going to go to sleep in front of a stranger, but I had no choice. Within what seemed like seconds, my eyes became heavy, and so did my head.

I could see visions running through my mind in almost in a blur. Showing me all of the faces of those people that were either killed or hurt at The Clarkton. Suddenly it didn't feel so bad. I wasn't sure if it was just the sleeping agent kicking in, or if I was starting to accept that, in this world, in this line of work, people simply died, and many were killed.

My head grew heavier as it slumped to the side. My eyes were barely able to stay open. This stuff worked fast. The pain that had returned was slowly fading away again. There was also a creeping blackness, as Jolin, Ember, and even the carriage began to vanish. Then there was nothing.

9

I screamed as I was shocked awake. My head was buzzing and my nose was burning on the inside, making it difficult to breathe. Jolin was moving another vial, this one yellow and thick, under my nose.

"This wakes you up, as you can see, Mr. Lox," Jolin said as he corked the liquid.

"No time to worry about that," Ember shouted as he handed me my dagger. "We got work to do."

He didn't seemed panicked, but then, Ember never did. Still, I knew him well enough to see something was wrong. He was quickly checking his bracers and greaves, making sure they were tight. It was something he usually didn't do unless he was about to engage a target. I was hoping that I was wrong, and that he was simply checking his armor, but in that same moment he checked his dagger and knives on his belt. I wasn't wrong.

It was hard to stay still now. I could feel the carriage moving faster than it had before, and as a result we were being bounced around a lot on the inside. It felt like we were trying to evade somebody, instead of simply driving to a location.

I peered out the window and saw a vastly different landscape than that of Thera. Where Thera had buildings and industry, this place had lush fields of green, gold, and brown, and trees as far as I could see. There were no tall buildings in view; instead there were farms, vast acres of grow shelters for food, and shelters for the livestock.

Most of the Prime Sovereignty received its produce

from Pradeep grow shelters. Crops couldn't be left to grow on their own naturally. The constant rain every night would hurt more than it helped. So would the snow in the day. To combat this, we had grow shelters, places like the one my mom worked in, where crops were grown, tended to, and harvested in controlled environments. We had been using grow shelters for as long as I could remember, and Pradeep had more than any other Kingdom.

The snow was still falling, but it had gotten darker outside; soon the rain would come. I must had been out for a while.

"Mr. Lox, welcome to Pradeep," Jolin said as he put himself into a little ball on the carriage floor. While Ember didn't look panicked, Jolin certainly did. He seemed jumpy; his words came out as stutters, and he had visible sweat on his brow and upper lip. This was not the same man who had approached us in The Clarkton with confidence.

I looked out the window once more to view the scenery of Pradeep and too see what had everybody so wound up, but this time I saw three arrows come flying by the carriage. I stood to lean over Jolin so I could look out the door slightly. Instantly I noticed my leg was feeling better. Glancing down at it, I could see it was still exposed, but the wound was clean and closed. The wound looked days old now, instead of hours. I made a mental note to get some of that stuff for myself after this job was complete.

Slowly, I opened the door to peek out.

"Careful," Ember said, pulling his hood up. Behind us I could see men pursuing our carriage. These men were bare chested, with long black hair that fell well below their shoulders, and snarls on their faces. Their muscles seemed unnaturally pronounced as they came closer into view. There had to have been at least ten of them, and they all rode fully-mature caprongs.

I could feel my face twist in surprise. I had never seen a mature caprong before. They were something you only heard about. The older a caprong, the harder they were to tame. That's why only young caprongs were used for service. The mature ones—they were menacing. Standing over six feet tall, with manes billowing in the air as they ran, and horns that stretched out over a foot long. These caprongs were nothing like the ones that pulled our carriages. These caprongs were out of nightmares.

All of the men had bows raised, except for the one in the front. He had no weapon at all, but he did have some sort of paint on his face and body, while the others didn't.

I shut the door and turned to Ember. "What happened?"

Ember tossed my cloak to me. From instinct alone, I put it on.

"Those are Pradeep border guards," Ember said to me. Thuds sounded around the carriage as he spoke. Arrows were slowly finding their mark, and a few actually pierced the carriage. Had Jolin not been on the floor, one would have hit him.

Pradeep border guards were known to be violent, and overly protective. They were not bound to the same rules as Pradeep city or palace guards. Here on the border, they had unparalleled freedom, and laws were more of a choice to them. They could either obey or do what they wanted freely. They made sure people from other kingdoms didn't cross Pradeep borders unannounced. They were mainly there to protect the grow shelters, and to engage possible attackers. Border guards were stationed at all entrances of Pradeep. I wasn't a worldly scholar, and even I knew this. How could Jolin not have known?

"You didn't know they would be here?" I asked him as he continued to lay on the floor, scared of our attackers.

"Our employer was supposed to handle passage into the kingdom. I don't know why they would be attacking us."

"Took your yolars and decided to kill us anyway," Ember said. "Well, I'm not going to hide in a carriage and wait for them to let one of those arrows hit our driver." Ember glanced out the window once more as the air around him shimmered for a split second, and then he was gone. This was turning out to be a long day.

I could see Ember now from where I was looking out the window.. He had appeared on a caprong behind one of the riders. In seconds his knife was buried into the rider's neck, and then he warped again. The rider fell off as his caprong stumbled and then began running off in a different direction. With no rider to control it, the caprong was free.

Reaching inside myself, I found my target and warped. The second of silence came, and then I found myself falling to the ground and rolling.

The impact as I collided with the ground hurt and knocked the air out of me. I had missed my target. Clearly, warping onto a moving caprong was harder that Ember had made it look. I could see the Pradeep border guards growing smaller as they chased after the carriage. Pushing myself off the ground, I warped again. I overdid it some, and this time I crashed into the back of a rider. Instantly, I began to fall off the caprong, but I grabbed the rider's hair and brought him down with me, making us both fall to the ground.

The rider got to his feet before me as he looked to his fallen bow and quiver. He reached for one of the arrows and attempted to stab me with it. I could have stayed to fight him, but I needed to catch the others before they were out of sight and I wouldn't be able to warp to them. As the guard slashed at me, I allowed my eyes to fall on the closest guard, still riding his caprong, that I could see. A slither of silence came again as I warped.

I knew this wasn't going to be a good warp, and I was ready for it. My feet hit the ground running and, instantly, I warped again. As I reappeared, I threw one of my knives and caught a caprong in its hind leg. I was actually trying to aim for the Pradeep border guard on top of the caprong, but it was hard to aim coming out of a warp. Hitting the caprong was better than missing altogether, I supposed.

The massive beast let out a howl as it stumbled to the ground, sending its rider along with it. The howl of pain sent a tremor across my body and made my body feel a chill. I actually felt bad for the caprong for a moment.

Ember was still going from guard to guard, leaving only four left. I ran and warped again. "Yes!" I screamed as I landed perfectly on a Pradeep rider's caprong. The rider looked over his shoulder at me, and I quickly delivered my elbow to his nose. Blood gushed from it as if it was a popped grape. Before he could react to his nose, I grabbed his long hair—there was just so much of it, and it felt oily—pulled it back, and delivered another elbow to his neck that sent him to the ground as well.

Reaching for the straps used to hold on to the caprong, I pulled myself up to where the rider had been. I'm not sure if it was from fear or the sheer excitement of riding a caprong, but I couldn't stop my hands from shaking, and my heart felt like it was about to explode in my chest. I'd never ridden a caprong before, and here I was now, riding a mature one. Close enough that I could touch the horns! If some of the elite nobles of Thera could have seen me then. The jealousy on their wealthy faces would have been worth the risk alone.

Wind pummeled my face, and I had to squint my eyes some just to see. It was only Ember, myself, and two other Pradeep guards chasing the carriage now.

"Carriage," I thought I heard, over the wind hitting my face.

Turning to my left, I saw Ember riding alongside me on top of a caprong.

"Get the carriage," he yelled as he pointed ahead of us. *The carriage?* I thought to myself. I looked up and saw that the carriage had detoured from the road, and it was quickly moving through a field. From where I rode, I could see the driver was no longer there. An arrow must had finally found him. For a second, I wondered where the body had fallen and why I hadn't seen it.

The caprong wouldn't catch the carriage. Not before it crashed, anyway. It was too far ahead. I was fairly sure I was going to die, but I had to try. I heard a scream from somewhere else close by. Ember was dispatching another guard. He would surely be more suited for this, but here I was. With teeth clenched so tight that my jaw hurt, I warped again, hoping to land on top of the carriage to regain control.

Naturally, yet again, I missed. I had intended to land on top of the carriage, but instead just missed it. As I reappeared, I could see the carriage moving away from under me. My fingers barely gripped the ledge as I extended my arms out. I was able to catch hold of the ledge, but my lower body slammed into the back of the carriage. It felt like a wall had just hit me in the stomach, and it took all the strength I had to hold on.

"Oh no," I said out loud, as I felt it hit my face, and then my hand. Between the warping, caprong-riding, and fighting for my life, somehow I hadn't noticed that the snow had stopped falling. The sky erupted as it began to rain. My fingertips were starting to slip.

"Whoa! Whoa!" I heard a voice yelling over the rain. It was Ember. I didn't know when or how, but he was on the carriage now.

His aim was better than mine, and he had control of the caprongs. The carriage was his now. Or it would be shortly. The downside—I was still slipping. I couldn't simply warp, because I was hanging and couldn't actually see the top of the carriage. I would likely just warp into the air, and come crashing down to the ground again.

Using as much strength as I could, I tried to pull myself up, placing my foot on a portion of the carriage for support. The falling rain had already done its part, and my foot slipped as the carriage jerked. With it went my hands and any grip I had had on the slippery carriage ledge. I began to fall. The ground came rushing up to me, and I could hear the carriage continue to run away as I prepared for impact.

10

"Keeper knows you're pathetic," Ember said as he stood over me. He kicked me in the side slightly, but I didn't move. I was in too much pain, and it was a soft kick.

He kicked me again, this time harder, and then extended his hand as I grunted.

"Get up. Rain's coming down unusually hard right now and I have no intentions of standing in it if I don't have to."

I reached for his hand and made my way off of the muddy ground.

The carriage was waiting close by, and from the looks of it, aside from a few arrows stuck in it, it had held up to the attack pretty well. I splashed through the new-forming puddles as I slowly walked to the carriage. Ember opened the door and lumbered inside as I glanced up to the driver seat. There, in his nice clothes, soaking wet, was Jolin. Clearly he hadn't planned on driving the carriage, or else he would have brought a cloak.

"Hurry it up, Lox," Ember shouted from inside the carriage.

He had left the door open as he waited for me, and apparently all of the action had made him thirsty. In his hand was a large bottle that he had likely gotten from the icebox, that contained a light brown, amber liquid. Ember's drink of choice was wine, but in a tight spot he made almost anything work.

I knew Ember would disagree with me, but I did feel bad slightly for Jolin, even though I probably shouldn't have. I cleared my throat a little too loudly to get his attention. Jolin turned and looked at me, his fine black hair stuck to his head and his wet clothes clinging to him.

"Ah, Mr. Lox," Jolin said, almost casually. "Glad to see you held your own with those guards."

"Take this," I said, removing my cloak and tossing it up to him. He caught it quickly, and began to put it on without hesitation.

"Thank you, Mr. Lox," he said with a slight nod. It wasn't a water resistant cloak, like the nobles had, but it would keep him dry for the remainder of the trip, however long that might be. Jolin stood up and placed his arm through the cloak. Despite Jolin being a little older than me, I was larger and taller than he was. He seemed almost childlike as he closed the larger cloak around him and put the hood up.

My back still hurt. So did my side, my pride, and my ego. Everything hurt, except for my recently cut leg, it seemed. I looked inside the carriage and. instead of walking those few feet, I warped. When I reappeared inside, I fell into the seat across from Ember, who was still drinking. He had finished a third of the bottle.

"Shut the door," he said as he leaned back and put his feet up. I leaned over and, as instructed, shut the carriage door. Jolin must had been listening, because as soon as the door shut, the carriage began to move.

Ember placed his bottle slightly to his side. "As soon as this is all over, first training session is warping to moving targets."

"I can understand that. It's a little difficult," I said as I adjusted in the seat to relieve some stress on my back. After that, I put my feet up too. It was comforting to see that the wounded area on my leg was still fine.

"No, I don't think you do," Ember said as he shook his

head. "It was horrible to even watch you attempt. Then, after you messed up the first time, you tried again, and yet again failed. As your teacher in the skill of warping, I almost wished one of those guards would have finished you off, just to stop the embarrassment."

I knew it may not had been as flashy as his attack, but I had still taken some of those guards down, and almost caught the carriage. Considering it was my first time, I'd thought it wasn't a bad display.

Before I could climb deeper into the self-pity of my mind, I realized we had begun to slow down. Looking out the window, I could see we had ventured deeper into Pradeep's lands. Beyond the fields, where some of its grow shelters were kept. Finally, the carriage stopped, and moments later a swift knock came to the door. Ember took a final gulp from his bottle and then left it on his seat as he opened the door.

Standing outside was, of course, Jolin. Ember hopped out and stood beside him. He stood there as rain continued to fall on him. He had removed my cloak and was holding it in his hand.

"Thank you, Mr. Lox," he said as I stepped down and took the cloak from him. "Follow me, gentlemen," Jolin said as he quickly turned and began walking. Ember followed and, as soon as my cloak was on, so did I. It smelled faintly sweet on the inside, now, after Jolin had worn it.

"Jolin, what's with the attitude?" Ember asked as he followed behind Jolin.

Jolin paused for a moment and stopped walking, then suddenly continued. "Attitude, Mr. Ember?" he asked.

"That's just what I mean. What's with the *Mr. Ember, Mr. Lox*, and so forth."

Jolin simply continued to walk, and was currently

leading us through what seemed to be a grow shelter graveyard.

"I learned at a young age, Mr. Ember, to respect everyone. Man, woman, child, nobleman, royalty, or commoner. In the Prime Sovereignty, social status is everything, and it can be taken from you at a moment's notice. A lesson I have witnessed firsthand. I find it easier to just treat everybody the same."

We turned around a bend. We were deep in this place now. Many abandoned grow shelters surrounded us. From the looks of them, they were old. Many had caved in on themselves, making them look as if some giant being had punched half of the building in. These, I would guess, were some of the first grow shelters ever made. They were shadows of the grow shelters used now, like the one my mother used to work in. These grow shelters had more steel and pipes, and less glass. Newer grow shelters were constructed of mostly glass, and had only steel frames to hold it all in place.

Why had Pradeep, or its royal family, simply allowed the ancient shelters to stay? Why not destroy them and build anew?

"Don't mistake me for a polite fool, though, Mr. Ember," Jolin said as he approached one of the smallest and most dilapidated grown shelters. "I still have my secrets. I am a Tongue, as you would say, and people tell me the most amazing things."

"I don't doubt that for a second," Ember replied.

"Here we are. For a moment I thought I was lost," Jolin said.

"Lost?" I asked him. "You didn't know where we were going?"

Jolin opened the large front door of the old grow

shelter. Surprisingly, it didn't make a sound. Not even a little creak from the metal. This was odd, considering that the surrounding buildings looked like they would make noise if you only looked at them too long. Somebody had gone out of their way to make sure our entry would go unnoticed.

"I had an idea," Jolin said as he walked inside. "But with the rain and approaching darkness, many of these buildings look the same. We don't have torches here, so let's just be glad we made it before nightfall came."

Ember waited and allowed me to go in first. He stood outside in the rain and looked at a neighboring grow shelter. He warped away for a moment, and then returned back to the door. "All clear," he said as he stepped inside and shut the door. He had warped to higher ground to make sure we weren't being followed, or, at the worst case, being set up.

Inside the grow shelter smelled different. One would expect the smell of dirt, maybe animal droppings, or even mildew, but instead it smelled clean. Just as with the door, somebody had done some work on the inside as well.

"Just up ahead," Jolin said as he pointed. From where we stood near the entrance were some steps that led down to a lower level, and a walkway that led directly in front of us. Whatever had once been at the end of the walkway was no longer there, because that portion of the building had collapsed and created a wall of debris. Aside from that, the remaining parts of the grow shelter looked to be in good shape.

We walked down the steps, every foot making loud clanking sounds on the metal. The steps had seen better days. They were completely rusted, and very small amounts of the metal were visible. At the bottom of the steps was a room that had the word *Division Head* on it, but many of the letters were faded. While it was getting darker around us, on the inside of this room, visible light peered from the cracks of the door's frame, and could be seen through the dirty glass. I could see what seemed to be two shadows moving.

I saw Ember's hand disappear, and followed suit. If this was some sort of elaborate setup, they wouldn't get the drop on us.

"So you finally, at long last, get to meet our enigmatic benefactors, Mr. Ember and Mr. Lox," Jolin said as he knocked on the door. "It's me," he said, as both of the moving shadows suddenly stopped moving. "I have them with me."

"Them?" I heard a male voice say from behind the door.

"Come in," a second voice called from behind the door. This voice was female, yet seemed stronger and more dominant than the male voice. Jolin turned the knob and opened the door. Ember glanced at me over his shoulder and gave me a slight nod as he mouthed the words, *be ready.*

The door swung open, and light from the burning lamps poured over us. Jolin walked in as Ember and I followed.

Two people stood at a large square table. There was a male holding a large, thick book. He looked like he could have been in his late twenties, and he was tall. Taller than me, but about the same height as Ember. He was thin, but not in a lean, muscular way; he had styled, dirty blonde hair, and a face that flaunted a stubble of the same color. His eyes seemed to be sunken in, as if he hadn't slept in days, and he was wearing common trousers and a shirt, but he looked out of place in them. Aside from his tired expression, everything about him screamed wealth, from his clean hands to his styled and trimmed hair.

To his right was a woman, who, while older, resembled him greatly. She was a little shorter than Jolin, and as she turned her head to look at each of us, her long blonde hair swayed from side to side. She truly was beautiful. She had blue eyes that seemed to flicker in the light of the lamp, high cheekbones, and a curvy figure. She, too, seemed out of place in her casual clothing.

"Keeper, it can't be," I heard Ember whisper under his breath slightly. What had he figured out that I hadn't? While these two before me looked familiar, I couldn't remember where I had seen them before.

Honestly, I didn't care who they were, to a certain extent. They had organized an ambush on Ember and I, an ambush that had almost gotten my leg chopped off, and just coming to meet them here had put us in danger. We were Warpers; we usually didn't encounter groups. The scope of our powers isn't as effective with multiple people coming at us.

I could feel my fist balling up, my chest heaving, and my breathing sounded louder than normal. It got worse the more I looked at these two, and I had had enough. I drew my dagger and took a step forward, but felt Ember quickly holding me back by my arm. My motion to attack wasn't missed by the others in the room, as they all flinched some as I took that step. Even Jolin reacted.

The woman's eyes were still wide, and she had taken a step back closer to the wall. As if that would have done any good. I didn't want to kill them; I couldn't have, even if I'd wanted to, because of the curse, but I was angry enough to want them to feel some sort of pain. Maybe the type of pain that you experience from a massive cut on the leg. That seemed fitting.

"Take it easy," Ember said to me with gritted teeth in more of a whisper.

I put my blade up and leaned back against the far wall of the room. I wanted to be as far from these people as I could.

Now that I had a full view of the room, I noticed something about it. It was clearly a place that hadn't got much use. Aside from the table, chairs, and the lamps, the room was completely empty. Spotless and clean, but empty.

Jolin walked to the table and pulled a chair from it. Sitting down, he removed some of his wet clothes and let them hit the floor beside him. "Much better," he said, as he sat, shirtless, and let his hands hover over one of the lamps on the table.

"What is this, Jolin?" the woman asked. "We asked you to fetch the man called Ember." "Nobody fetches me. I don't care who you are. Speak that way about me again, as if I'm a hound, and you will have more to worry about than him," Ember said as he pointed at me. "And he won't be able to hold me back, I assure you.".

"What my sister means," the tall man said, "is that we asked you to bring us Ember, and you bring him, plus another. What is the meaning of this, Jolin?" He spoke with a slight accent. They both did, but his words were more soothing. Not like Jolin's ability, but he spoke as if he were addressing a council instead of two killers.

These two were definitely used to giving orders and having people fear or respect them.

"We needed a Warper for the job," Jolin replied. "We'll now we have two. Mr. Ember, and his pupil, Mr. Lox" Jolin pointed to me as he said my name. Both the man and woman stared at me with a blank expression for a second.

"Two Warpers," the woman finally said, as she looked at the man who was her brother.

"This is interesting indeed," the man said as he sat down and opened his book. He seemed to be reading. Was he that carefree that he would rather read right now?

I had had enough of being left out of the loop, and the more they spoke, the more my fingers began to drum on the handle of my blade. I could feel the vein pulsing in my neck, and if I looked at them silently any longer, I felt like I was going to glare a hole into them. So I finally spoke.

"Who are you two?" I asked. "After that stunt at The Clarkton, I at least deserve to know who was responsible for me almost losing a leg."

"That was her idea," the man said as he continued to flip pages in his book. "I never agreed with it, honestly." The lady stiffened as my eyes met hers.

"Who they are," Ember chimed in, "are nobles. High nobles. Rema Thorne, and her younger brother Remy. In Thera, these two are heads of a noble family that wield as much power as royalty."

A wave of knowledge hit me as hard as the ground I had fallen on earlier. That's why I knew I had seen them before. Thera was the only kingdom without a royal family, because the Emperor himself governed us. The Thorne family were his closest associates, and often did things on his behalf. No wonder Ember was told this job would pay well. Why would they, of all people, have a job that required me, Ember, and Jolin?

As if he was in my head, Ember asked what I had just thought.

"What I want to know is why one of the richest and most well-known families in all of the five kingdoms has a job for a Tongue and a pair of Warpers?"

Just at that moment, another knock came at the door.

11

Instantly, Ember and I drew our daggers again. Jolin perked up at the table, while Remy continued to read his book.

"No doubt, that is the last member of our crew," he said as his sister slowly walked to the door. I don't think she wanted to move too quickly because of our drawn daggers. I couldn't blame her. From what I had gathered, Ember trusted these people about as little as I did. With that lack of trust, however, came a large amount of curiosity.

As the door opened, a tall man slowly limped in under the aid of a cane. He had pale skin, a long hooked nose, and thick gray hair on the sides, but was bald up top. I had never seen so many wrinkles on one face before. His robes were dragging on the floor as he slowly turned to place a hand on the door knob. I thought he was going to shut the door behind him, but then he looked at us and spoke.

"Who are these three?" he asked, in a voice that was very raspy. He sounded like he had sand in the lining of his throat.

"These are the other people who will be joining us," Rema said. She pointed to us individually as she spoke our names.

"The shirtless one sitting is Jolin." Jolin waved with energy at the old man. The old man grunted at Jolin, but didn't speak. "Jolin is a Tongue, he will be invaluable on this job," Rema continued.

The old man slowly shifted his glance to us.

"These two are Ember and Lox, our Warpers.

Naturally they will do the dirty work when the time comes," Rema said.

"You told me that there would be two others, not three," the old man said as he continued to hold the knob of the door. After thinking for a moment, he slowly closed it.

"We assumed there would be," Remy continued. "I assure you, we didn't expect two Warpers for the price of one, but here we are, Vida."

Vida? So the old man was called Vida. An unusual name for a man in his sixties.

"In any case," Rema said, "an extra Warper can only help our cause."

Vida looked at us all slowly, as if he was pondering what to do. If I were him, I'd have just left. What could a man of his age, a man who could barely walk upright, offer on whatever this mystery job was?

It was at that very moment that the old man did something unexpected. He tossed his cane to Jolin, who caught it in the air with his brow raised. Now, the man was standing upright.

"So this is the gang then. Some high nobles, a Tongue, and two Warpers?" Vida said, but in a voice not his own. Even Ember's mouth dropped open at this.

Vida, who moments ago had had a voice that sounded like stones rubbing together, now had the voice of a younger female.

"What in the hell?" I said, moving closer to Vida slightly. Jolin simply looked at Vida, and then he glanced at the stick in his hand.

"Mr. Remy, Ms. Rema?" Jolin said, as he looked to them for answers. Neither of them said a word. Instead, they grinned at each other, and then back to Vida.

As the old man moved, his hand changed. And then,

not just his hand, but his entire body. Clothes and all. While he had been, moments ago, standing six feet tall, he now began to shrink to a little over five and a half feet. The balding head adjusted, and the gray hair on the sides seemed to retract into his skull and become short and black.

"Changeling," Ember said as he stepped back.

As Vida smiled at us, the old face of the man began to contort and change. The wrinkles and pale white face began to fade away and were replaced by smooth, light brown skin. The old and sunken eyes were replaced by vibrant round ones of a honey-brown color. The thin, dry, cracked lips, weathered by years of age, began to expand. In their place were the round, perky lips of a young woman.

Even the clothes, the long dusty robe, changed into a form-fitting pair of trousers that revealed a strong frame. Up top, a white shirt, worn by many women from the Walden kingdom.

The changing stopped, and now, before us, where a man ravaged by time had once stood, there was instead a woman. Perhaps one of the prettiest I had ever seen. That aside, I had no idea what I had just witnessed.

"Where in the all the Kingdoms did you find a Changeling?" Ember asked slowly.

"This Changeling has a name," the woman snapped as she went to sit down in the chair across from Jolin, who still hadn't moved since the change had started.

"This is Vida Orax," Rema said as she stood beside Vida and placed a hand on her shoulder. "Judging from the looks on your faces—" She looked to me and then back to Jolin. "I'm guessing some explaining is in order. Vida is—"

"I can speak for myself," Vida said as she removed Rema's hand from her shoulder.

She was a feisty one, clearly. She had fire inside her.

Maybe it was the years with Ember that made me admire this fire, but I was beginning to like her already.

"Hey—Lox, was it?" she said to me as I came back to reality. "You mind not smiling at me in such a creepy way?"

I felt Ember nudge me in the side.

"Either of you know what a Changeling is?" Vida asked, as she slid her chair back some in order to put her feet on the table. "I know you do," she said as she pointed to Ember. "You two—" She waved a finger to me and Jolin. "Not so much."

She adjust her feet on the table and placed her hands behind her head.

"The Keeper, just like he did with all of you, saw fit to make me a Changeling. Able to change my appearance into any person I have seen in my lifetime."

Oh, no. Not her too. Was I the only person alive in The Prime Sovereignty who didn't believe in The Keeper?

"Changelings are incredibly rare," Ember said out loud to the group. "Rarer than Warpers, and we are rare."

"You're right," Vida said as she stood and walked over to Ember. He had almost a foot of height on her. As she got closer to us, I could feel my skin beginning to tingle. "So you're Ember. I thought you'd be bigger."

"You've heard of me?" Ember said with a slight smile.

"Before I got into this line of work, I lived on the streets of Walden, Pradeep, and Thera for four years, and every major death was attributed to you. Some of which I'm not even sure *were* yours. They didn't all mention you by name, of course, but they all would say it was a Warper. Some said the name Ember."

She turned and looked at me up and down. "Never heard of you, though."

"He's my student," Ember said defensively. I don't

know why, but for the first time, hearing him introduce me as his student made me feel like less of a man.

"Clearly," Vida said.

"So, wait," Jolin said as he stood up. "I'm a Tongue, but only an inward Tongue. So people are forced to tell me the truth when I want them too. Then there are rare people who are outward Tongues— people forced to tell the truth to anybody they speak to. Those poor bastards."

He pointed over to Ember.

"You just referred to yourselves as inward Warpers, and I've seen you warp. Are you saying that there are outward Warpers too? People able to warp others, but not themselves?"

"It doesn't work that way," Remy said, as Rema sat down at another chair beside the table. Before he could finish, he was silenced by a glare from Ember.

Ember cleared his throat. "Lox, I'll let you explain."

"Oh, ah." I froze for a moment as every eye in the room turned to me. "Warpers like us," I said, as I made a weird hand gesture between Ember and myself, "can Warp ourselves to anyplace in our direct line of sight. Outward Warpers can only warp things outside of them and in their line of sight. So an outward Warper could warp your yolar bag from your hands and into his own as long as it's in his line of site. But that same outward Warper can't warp other people. No Warper can do that."

"Man," Jolin said. "Imagine the secrets, the food, anything a person could steal as an outward Warper."

"And they do," I added.

Jolin stopped rubbing his chin hair and looked at me.

"He's right," Remy said. "Almost half of the items stolen in the five kingdoms are due to outward Warpers; that's why they aren't allowed in yolar mines. Inward

Warpers are rare—hence the surprise, that you showed up with two tonight. Outward Warpers are almost as common as rats or caprongs."

I eyed Vida for a moment, and she, in return turned her face up at me. I was beginning to think that maybe she had too much fire inside her.

Jolin returned to his seat and looked directly to Vida.

"What?" she asked.

"Ms. Vida," Jolin began, as Vida exhaled loudly. "I'm going to assume that, like us, you are an inward Changeling, and, as such, that there are outward changelings, able to change things, but not people?"

"No," Vida said as she shook her head. "I'm an inward Changeling, but outward Changelings can only change other people, not items. Plus, the person changed is permanently changed, and can't be changed back. I've heard stories that, if an outward Changeling dies, those they changed would revert back, but I don't know how valid that is. It's very confusing when we talk about it like this," she said as she shook her head.

"A person running around the kingdoms changing people hardly seems useful," Jolin said.

"It's not," Vida said. "Outward Changelings are almost extinct. I have only met one in my nineteen years."

"Not that I don't enjoy getting Mr. Respectful here caught up on the way some of us are deemed special by The Keeper, but I'm here to make yolars," Vida said, a little forcefully. "You said if I did this job, I'd never have to be a spy for hire again."

"The moment of truth has arrived, sister," Remy said as he clasped his fingers together and looked at Rema. "Go ahead and tell them this job of yours."

She stood from the table and rubbed his head, as if he

was a child. "Please ignore my brother. He is smart, and loves to read his books of fantasy and science, but he lacks vision and the nerve to do what must be done." The smile on Remy's face faded some.

"This is why I'm the head of the family.

"The Prime Sovereignty, as you know, consists of the five Kingdoms. All of which are surrounded by Water. In this world, we are but a tiny portion. Do any of you know why we don't know what is beyond our waters? What's beyond the Kingdoms?"

"Nothing," I answered firmly. I was surprised I was the first to answer. I hated myself for what I was about to say, but I said it anyway. "Supposedly, if you believe in such things, there was a war that ravished the lands. A war between gods and men, and The Keeper, in his mercy, created what we call the Prime Sovereignty, for people to start anew. So there is nothing beyond our waters."

Vida clapped her hands.

"He is right. We all know the stories. We were taught them at an early age. But what if they were lies?" Rema said. "Recently, a man was discovered on the shores of Galcon, who had never been here before. He arrived on a vessel that he called a boat."

"A boat?" Jolin said. "What a silly name for a vessel."

"He was the only survivor of five people on this boat. After the Emperor found out that he was from some unknown place, he had him killed, and the bodies, along with the boat, were burned and buried. This was months ago. Now people have been disappearing. All around the Prime Sovereignty, and none notice, because Warpers are assumed to be behind it."

"Figures," Ember said.

"What does this have to do with the job?" Vida asked.

"In short," Rema replied, "everything. I believe the Emperor is abducting these people and, for some reason or another, is secretly sending them out into the water to see what's beyond."

She turned to look at Remy and cleared her throat. He looked at her with an unusual expression on his face, and sighed.

"We have proof," Remy said.

"We don't really care about proof. You need a person taken care of, we will do it," Ember said. "But I honestly don't know why we need the help of a Tongue and a Changeling spy."

Rema and her brother locked eyes for a moment before she faced us all.

"Because the person we must kill is one we also must obtain secrets from, and we will likely need the help of a spy to get close to him."

She paused for a moment.

"We are going to kill the ruler of this land and lord of the five kingdoms."

My heart suddenly found its way sinking into my stomach as she spoke. I looked at Ember. Surely she didn't mean what I thought

. She continued to speak.

"The Immortal, the man who has risen from the dead, again and again. We will find a way to permanently kill Emperor Anavor Nal."

PART II

12

Rema had given us two days to consider her job offer, and if we wanted in, we were to meet them in a secondary home they owned in Thera.

The next two days went by rather fast after that. I thought it was insane, but the rest of the so-called team didn't seem to think so. Ember, Jolin, and even Vida all seemed to embrace the challenge. Ember just wanted the payday; he already had the fame. Jolin and Vida, however, were hard to figure out.

Vida, I guessed, wanted the payday like Ember. There was no need for fame or infamy if you were to continue to be a spy. I felt that Jolin wanted something more. I wasn't sure what, but I had the feeling that he had a secondary agenda that none of us knew about. Something about him was still a mystery. I could almost sense it.

The time was approaching to meet the others, and I was currently standing on a high building as the snow fell, watching my home. I had warped in when my mom and the twins were gone to drop my remaining yolars off to them. Four bronze, a few silvers, and a handful of gold. The four bronze yolars alone could get them by for a few months.

My mom and I had talked about this. If ever a time came when I was gone more than usual, the money was for her to spend wisely for herself and the twins, just in case it was a last payment. When she saw the amount, she would know I was up against something I may not make it back from.

I waited a few more minutes before I actually was able

to get a glimpse of them. My mom was slowly walking with a bag from the market in one hand, and she had the twins on her opposite side. Luka was skipping and holding Kula's hand, while Kula held on to our mother's hand. They all formed a chain of sorts, but it kept them together. They were all happy, they were all smiling, and it made me feel good to see them, just in case it was the last time.

I wanted to go speak to them, but Ember had insisted I didn't. That this would prepare me, keep me strong. He believed that, one day, I wouldn't have him, and that the enemies I would create as my own legend grew could find those close to me and use them against me. It was the reason he, and many of our kind, never married or had families. His insistence on this also went to prove that he truly thought this job was within our grasp.

I prepared myself to warp away, and then, suddenly, my mom stopped walking. I didn't know if she could feel me watching, or if it was just a mother's intuition, but she paused, and, of all the buildings around, she turned to her left and looked in my direction. From where she stood, I was three stories up, so I could be seen, but I was more a large dot than a figure she could make out. Yet still she looked, placed her bag on the ground gently, and gave a little wave in my direction, and then placed her free hand over her heart.

It was how she'd once told Nowrt that she loved him when they worked together and she couldn't shout out loud around people. After a moment, she stooped down to grab her bag and continued into our little house.

"I love you too, Mom," I said as I put my hood up, turned, and then warped away.

Normally I would warp to Ember's place and wait for him before we went to the meeting location provided by the

Thornes, but in this case I couldn't because he had to get Sprits, and then find a normal means of travel, because he couldn't warp with Sprits. Rema had insisted that, until the job was over, we all would live together in the home they could provide, but I wasn't sure why.

Her brother, oddly, was against this. In our Pradeep meeting, he had literally stood up and almost begged her not to do this, but she had refused. Saying that it must happen.

Rema was clearly the brawn of the duo. Remy was the brains. He consumed the books he read like a child eating sweets. In the meeting alone he had read almost two full books. One on the history of the five kingdoms, and another on why some animals acted the way they did. Two totally different books, both of which were thicker than a caprong's leg.

I finally warped to our designated meeting place. This additional home that the twins owned. It must have been nice, to have such wealth that you had multiple homes for no reason. Ember had homes in other kingdoms, but they were more like shells. A building with walls and the bare essentials on the inside. This house I stood before, however, was nothing short of intimidating.

When I was told where it was in Thera, it was a dead giveaway to the amount of wealth the Thornes truly possessed. The closer I walked to the house, the more bicycles I saw. Moments ago up the street I had seen a group of kids on them. Kids, no older than Kula and Luka, with their own bicycles. The most expensive mode of transportation your yolars could purchase, and these people were using them as a child's plaything. Half of a city could eat off of the wealth these children played on.

Another thing that was odd about the location of the

house was that it was literally a few warps away from the Emperor's palace.

I walked up to the front of the house and stood near the door. I was instructed not to draw attention to myself, so I tried my best to keep my weapons covered, and I even wore my hood down, since the snow that was falling wasn't heavy. Most of all, I couldn't warp inside or close to the house. I was instructed to simply knock on the door, which I did.

As I waited, I took a few steps back to take the entire place in. It looked massive, and yet this wasn't the main house. The Thornes' main home was easily three times the size of this, and was the second-largest building in Thera.

This house was three stories high, and seemed just as wide. There were stone statues on both sides of the door that had golden faces. The statues had the bodies of men, yet had faces that were simply stone.

Each window was outlined in a bright blue frame, which was a vivid contrast to the actual brown color of the building. I couldn't warp inside, even if I wanted to. I couldn't see inside. Each window had a thick curtain of some sort hanging in front of it, leaving little to see. At least we would be getting privacy.

My hand knocked on the door once more, but a little harder this time. In seconds the knob turned and swung open.

Standing before me was a rather short man, with a solid stocky frame. His arms seemed too short for his body, and his head seemed too big. He had a thick red mustache on his lip and a head full of curly red hair to match. His glasses were unusually thick and sat loosely on his nose.

Outside of his odd appearance, this man was dressed from head to toe in black. His trousers were black, his elegant shirt was black, and so were the square shaped shoes he wore.

"Yes?" the man said as he looked up at me.

"My name's Lox."

"Oh, yes, the Warper," the man said casually, and louder than I'd have wanted him to. "Yes. Yes. Right this way." He stood to the side and gestured for me to walk in.

I heard the door shut behind me as I took a few steps in. For as massive as it was, this place was practically empty. The first few rooms I walked through as I followed this man were completely empty.

Even the kitchen was empty. No tables, no chairs, no ice box, nothing at all.

"Ignore this kitchen. Meals are prepared in another one," the man said as he continued to lead me through the home. I could feel my brow rise as I let the words sink in. The house had two kitchens. Wow.

I followed this man up some steps, and to a large set of double doors. He knocked twice, and then opened one of them for me to enter. "In we go."

"Thanks," I said as I walked by him. I felt a little better when I saw the familiar faces inside.

Actually, it seemed as if I was last to arrive. Even Ember was here already, and he had had to walk, not warp. This room had furniture, and nice furniture at that. There were various tables around that all seemed larger than life. A few couches, one of which Jolin relaxed on, near a burning fire place, and then there was a massive table in the middle, directly in front of what looked like a chalk board.

At the center table was Ember, sitting down, with Sprits resting at his feet; Remy Thorne was to his left with yet another book; Vida was across from them, with her elbow on the table, allowing her head to rest in her hand; and Rema herself was standing near the board with chalk in her hand.

"I see you met Quarts, the caretaker of this home," Rema said as she smiled. Remy glared at her for some reason for this, and then returned to his book. As I walked to the table, Jolin casually waved his hand at me and then sat up from the couch and leaned so he could see the chalkboard.

"So we are all here," Rema said, as she began writing each of our names on the board, except for her brother's. "Ember, you're the legendary killer among us. Please tell the rest of us—when you have a job, what's the first thing you do?"

Ember inhaled deeply and nudged me in the side. "Go ahead and answer her, boy. You know this stuff just as much as me."

The eyes in the room shifted from Ember to me all at once. Vida looked at me. She seem irritated at first; then she gave me a slight smile, and I could feel my face getting hot. I felt that I lingered on her eyes too long after that, so I shifted my gaze to Rema's.

"You find out about your target first," I replied. "But in this case, we already know about him, and we know that he will be a hard person to kill."

"Go on," Rema said, as if she was teaching a child how to spell.

"Then you do recon. See where they go, who they know, what makes them tick, and try to find a way in. You submerge yourself in their life for as long as it takes until you know everything about them."

Ember slapped me hard on the back. "Well put," he said as he leaned over to play with Sprits some.

"Lox is right," said Rema "We know about the Emperor, but we need more. We need to know about his home, his life, even his wife, the Empress."

I had forgotten about her. Empress Selen Nal was more of an afterthought. Her husband overshadowed her enough by simply being the Emperor.

She was more of a figurehead with a title. In fact, her only responsibility was to give the Emperor an heir, which she hadn't yet. She was much younger than her husband, becoming his wife at the age of sixteen, while he was in his forties. She was often said to be the reason he had become less brutal.

During the last war, during which Galcon, Pradeep, and Walden had tried to conquer Thera and split it among themselves, the Emperor had been ruthless. Killing men, women, and even the children who got in his way. As Thera began to lose the war, he had died for the first time. Six arrows to the chest from some Pradeep soldiers. When he resurrected later and was seen for the first time, he seemed almost like a different man. It was whispered that coming back from the dead had made him so weak that for the first few days he had isolated himself to gain his strength back. When he finally returned, he was his normal self, but not as murderous. He used other means to win the war. Some even said he had created monsters to serve him in secret, and Empress Selen was by his side the entire time, even at her young age. This was over twenty years, ago and now she still ruled by his side.

"Ms. Rema, I assume you have a plan?" Jolin said from the couch.

She eyed him slightly and then smiled. "I do. We go to a ball."

Jolin stood up quickly and clapped his hands together.

"I love going to balls. I haven't been to one since I was a kid," Jolin said as Vida removed her hand from her head and looked at him.

"You went to balls as a child?" Vida asked. Jolin froze for a few seconds as the room looked at him. His eyes darted as he tried to figure out what to say. "Yeah," he said, lowly, as he sat back down.

"Why a ball?" I asked Rema..

"The Emperor loves having them, for whatever reason, and he always has them at his palace. Usually, only royals and nobility attend, but this time, you all will." Rema turned to write under the names on the board. "Jolin, you will be playing the role of my servant."

Jolin exhaled, but otherwise didn't respond. Rema wrote the word *servant* under his name. "Lox, you and Vida will play the role of my wealthy friends. So you two will be acting as dates for each other. You will mingle, and when you are able, you will separate and search the palace for any information you can find."

She wrote under our names as well. I glanced at Vida, who seemed emotionless towards this entire plot. I tried to remain as casual as possible, but inside I was happier than expected.

"Finally, Ember, you will play the role of my date."

Ember let out a gruff sound.

"As we dance and interact, Jolin will casually talk to guests to learn their secrets. You just keep an ear open for anything that may aid in our plans. See? Simple yet fun reconnaissance."

"Reconnaissance isn't meant to fun or simple," Ember said, but Rema acted as if she couldn't hear him. Instead, she dropped the chalk down and wiped her hands as she looked at us.

"When is this ball? I assume we have to get clothes and things," I asked.

"The clothing of a noble will be given to you three," Rema said. "Vida can, well, *change* with her abilities."

At that moment, Quarts walked in with hands full of clothes.

"Time is of the essence, gentlemen," Rema said as she walked towards the door and left.

Remy removed himself from the meeting at the table. When he left, he had seemed angry, but I was starting to believe he was angry towards his sister.

"You three may want to hurry and find some clothes," Remy said.

"Why? How many days to we have before the ball?" I asked him.

"None, actually," Remy replied as he wiped his brow with the back of his hand. "It's tonight."

13

It took me a while to actually find clothes that fit well, so Ember and Jolin got ready before I did. It was apparent that Remy wasn't coming. He said he had to been going to balls since he was four, and that missing one was something he had no problem dealing with.

The clothes of a noble felt different. The way I moved in them was a little more constricting than a cloak and trousers, and I felt naked without my bracers and greaves on for protection. I had tried to keep them on, under the clothes, but it had become too tight and showed through the outfit. I was able to hide a throwing knife on each of my legs, though. Even with them there, I still preferred a dagger, but this would have to do.

Outside of those two weapons, I was bare. I had on a fitted black pair of pants, a fitted blue shirt made out of a very shiny, soft material, and perhaps the shiniest pair of shoes I had ever seen.

As I walked down the steps, I saw that Ember and Jolin were already waiting side by side and talking. Ember was getting along better with Jolin than when we had first met; for that matter, so was I. It took meeting the Thornes to see that he was just following his orders, as he had said.

Ember was dressed almost identically to me, except that he had a large top hat, a pale red shirt, and a cane. I was secretly jealous of the cane because, much like Ashland's, it had a secret dagger hidden on the inside. If he needed to, he could separate the cane and have an almost full-length sword at the ready. I had gotten a chance to examine it before we got dressed, and it was almost perfect in design. Ember had decided to keep it, and I couldn't blame him.

Jolin, however, wasn't dressed as nicely. Since he was to play the part of a servant, his clothes were more basic. Nothing was shiny, and nothing felt like bliss on the skin. Jolin had on a pair of trousers and a shirt with buttons, both of which were brown. He also had on some brown shoes and a pair of solid white gloves.

"Mr. Lox, the clothing of a noble fits you well," Jolin said as he looked down at himself. "Sadly, I am dressed as a high servant. My parents would be proud," he added with a grimace.

Ember adjusted his shirt. "I don't know why you're complaining. Between the three of us, I'm sure you are the most comfortable."

Jolin nodded in agreement.

"Where are Rema and Vida?" I asked as I peered outside through one of the windows. At the front of the house was parked yet another carriage. This one was bigger and nicer even than the one Jolin had picked us up in. The Thornes must have had a fleet of them.

"Not sure," Jolin said. "We are running out of time, though. The snow will stop soon, and none of us wants to be traveling in the rain." Jolin glanced at me slightly. "I never got a chance to ask you, Mr. Lox, but how is your leg doing?"

I moved my leg around a little and then extended it the best I could in the tight pants. "It's good. Between your mysterious vials and stitch-work, you may have saved the day."

Jolin smiled and did a fancy bow, as a servant would. "I live to serve, Mr. Lox," he said, with a slight laugh, which, in turn, made me laugh a little too.

As I stood next to Ember, I looked him in the face. He caught the expression and quickly avoided my eye.

"Did you trim your beard?" I asked him as I reached to grab his face.

"If that hand touches me, Keeper as my witness, I'll take it," he said as he stepped away. "And yes. I had too. Remy suggested it so that I would fit in among the nobles and royals."

His usual thick, woolly beard was gone, and what was left was the smooth shadow of a beard. "Now shut up," Ember said as he cleared his throat and adjusted his shirt.

At that moment Rema and Vida made their way down the steps. Rema seemed completely at ease in her long white dress and tall shoes. The dress had stones on the side that lead down to the front in a spiral that reflected from the light of the lamps in the room.

She looked almost magical. He hair was done in curls, and her lips were a vibrant red. She looked like true nobility—but while she was pretty, Vida was so much more.

Vida herself didn't have to find a an outfit. Because she was a changeling, she could simply alter her appearance. For a moment I had wondered if the Vida I was used to seeing was even the true *her*.

The dress she had created for herself was the exact same color of blue as my shirt, so when we stood beside each other, people would know we were together. Her dress hugged her body and made almost every curve she had, slight or major, seem to pop. Her hair she had kept the same. It was close-shaven on the sides, but longer and slightly reddish on the top. Her hair was definitely a unique style in the kingdoms, but I liked it. It was different, it was adventurous, and it seemed to fit her.

She didn't wear any makeup, but she didn't really need

to. Her skin was as flawless and as smooth as the shirt I was wearing. I could feel myself getting warm as she approached. It was clear that I had a thing for Vida Orax, and I was completely lost at how to handle that. Throwing a knife while warping from a building—that I could do. Talk to a woman without breaking into a sweat—not so much.

"Well, do we look nice," Rema said as she looked at Ember, Jolin and I. Jolin moved to respond, but before he could, Rema placed her small bag in his hand. "Jolin, be a dear and get the door. We may as well get in character."

My upper lip twitched as I held in a laugh while Jolin looked down at the bag and grabbed the door.

Ember extended his arm to Rema, who allowed her arm to lock inside his. They walked through the door and out into the carriage. The carriage door, too, was being held open by the driver. I could only assume he was a real servant, and not simply in character, like Jolin.

"You look nice," I said to Vida, as I extended my arm out to her. She looked down at my arm for a moment. I was afraid she was going to ignore it and walk away. She let out a little sigh, and then locked her arm inside of mine. As our skin touched, it took a lot for me to not to stumble towards the door being held open by Jolin.

"Happy hunting," I heard a voice call from above the stairs.

Over my shoulder, I could see Remy Thorne, standing above the stairs.

"Be careful," he said with a solemn look on his face. I nodded to him, and then walked out the front door and to the carriage, followed by Jolin.

We arrived at the ball just as the snow faded and was replaced by rain. I had seen the palace before, because it was in the middle of Thera, so warping by it happened on a regular basis. I just never had been this close to it. Never could I imagine a building being so large for only a single family.

It seemed that only Jolin and I were in amazement as we walked through the front entrance of the Palace. I knew Ember hadn't been here before, but he was good at hiding emotion and reactions. Rema, as a high noble, had been here plenty of times. As for Vida, I wasn't sure.

As we followed Ember, Jolin, and Rema, I leaned over and whispered in Vida's ear. "First time in the palace?"

She didn't even turn to me as she spoke. "No," she replied back dryly.

Once we made it past the first entrance, which seemed to be just a drop-off point, we were greeted by servants to the Emperor, who began to lead us to our table.

"Rema Thorne, the Keeper created you simply to be beautiful and admired," a random man said from across the floor as we walked by. Rema glanced in his direction as he waved and held up his glass. She smiled slightly and waved back.

We continued to walk past people. Music filled the main hall we were in, and some simply mingled, while others were dancing the time away. It was more crowded than I had ever expected, which would work in our favor when it came time to sneak away.

"Rema! Rema, dear," a woman shouted as she came over, followed by a trio of other women. They blocked our paths. "Hello, Amelia," Rema said, with a smile that was clearly forced. She didn't even acknowledge the other women around her.

"Well, who is this?" Amelia asked in a nasally voice as she looked at Ember. Amelia was clearly a noble, considering that her dress was elegant, and she had more jewels on her neck and ears than almost anyone could ever afford.

"This is Clips," Rema said. "My date for the evening." I hadn't been aware that we were using false names, and from how Ember's brow was raised, neither was he. Then again, we should have expected that. While his face wasn't well known, many had heard the name *Ember*.

"Oh, and what do you do, Clips?" Ember began to move his mouth, but Rema casually placed a slight kiss on his lips, which made him pause. My eyes grew wide at this and Jolin coughed.

"Clips owns land in Kameace, Galcon, and Walden. Used for farming and yolar mines," Rema said with a slight shrug of the shoulder. "He is a lover like none I have experienced before. The Keeper truly blessed this one."

"Wow," I said under my breath.

"Well, I do what I can," Ember said casually. Then he followed up with a slight tip of his hat to the three women standing behind Amelia. One of them actually blushed.

"We really must get to our table, Ms. Thorne," Jolin said from the side.

"Yes, Jolin, you are right. Amelia, ladies, I'm sure I'll see you again soon," Rema said as she leaned in and gave Amelia a fake kiss on the cheek, smiling at the women behind her.

When we finally found our table, Vida burst out laughing.

"That was awesome," she said, trying to contain herself.

"Those four will be making their way around the ball now, to talk about what just happened. If I know the people here like I think I do, they will want to come and see for themselves, and then we will unleash Jolin on them," Rema said, with a wink to Jolin, who was standing by the table.

Servants didn't sit with their masters, apparently. From where we were sitting, we had a grand view of what was going on around us. The people dancing and talking were only a part of it. There were people performing throughout the entire hall. A large portion of the side wall was dedicated to food. Massive amounts of food on a table that stretched the entire length of the hall so that, no matter where you were, food was close by. There was an identical table nearby with drink and wine on it. Ember seemed to have already set his sights set on this table.

"You two must play the part," Rema said as she leaned over to Vida and I.

"Play the part?" I asked, and Vida's face turned up.

"Well, it's clear that Jolin is my servant, since he hasn't left my side, and I have already laid the story for Ember. That just leaves you two. Act like you like each other. Go dance or something." Rema turned her head and lifted a glass of wine from close by.

I glanced at Vida, who bit her lower lip for a moment, shook her head, and then got up from the table. I thought she was simply leaving until she extended her hand to me.

"Try not to step on my feet too much, please," she said as I glanced up at her.

"Good luck boy," Ember said, as he, too, started on a glass of wine.

Once we were on the dance floor, surrounded by others, I froze.

"What's wrong?" Vida asked as she looked around.

"I don't really know what to do," I said, avoiding her eye.

She let out a little exhale, but smiled as she did so. "Just put your arm around my waist and take my hand," she said as she stepped in close. I didn't need to be told twice. I wrapped my arm around her and then found her free hand with mine. "Now, just follow my lead, and try not to—ouch!"

"Sorry," I said as I looked down.

As the moments went by, I began to get a hang of this dancing thing. Vida was pretty good at it, too.

"How are you such a good dancer?" I asked her. She kept looking around the dance hall, and finally looked up at me.

"I lived on my own for so long. It made me tough, but made me a little sharp around the edges, too."

"A little?" I asked with a grin. I felt her foot step on mine, a little too strongly to be an accident.

"Well, when I left the street life and began working as a spy, I knew I would eventually end up in a kingdom, and I'd have to dance. So I learned."

"You knew you'd have to dance to be a spy?" I asked.

She shook her head. "Not like that. I mean, the only people worth spying for or keeping secrets on are people with power. I'm sure Jolin would agree to that point. And for some reason, people with power love getting together at parties to show each other how powerful or rich they are. It was the best way to fit in."

She made sense, and we certainly were getting the benefits of it now.

"What about you?" she asked as we spun around in a circle and she leaned back in a dip motion.

"Not big on dancing?"

"I never needed to know how," I said. "My family didn't have money, or any reason to dance. Too tired from work, I suppose. Then, once I learned what I was—training to be a killer leaves little time for dancing."

"I suppose you're right," she said.

The music suddenly stopped, and everybody shifted their gaze to the front of the hall. The embrace I had on Vida faded as we both turned around. Being the guests of high nobility, we were seated near the exact same spot that people were looking at, but because we were dancing, we had an obscured view.

"Come on. We need to get closer," I said as I leaned and grabbed Vida's hand. I shuffled my way towards the front, where people were looking, while, behind me, I could hear Vida using a more verbal approach to get people to move. For some reason, I enjoyed hearing her curse at nobility.

We finally made it through the crowd and were able to see the table that everyone was looking at. Behind the table were two massive throne-like chairs, and several normal chairs beside them. The thrones seemed to be made entirely out of bronze. The sheer amount of time it must have taken to find so much bronze to make two such massive thrones was scary to me. I wondered how many people had slaved away in the mines, just for bronze, the most precious metal in the kingdoms, just for the Emperor to sit on.

Everybody who was sitting at a table stood up, and our table followed. Slowly, in walked a woman with a thin frame and long red hair that fell to her lower back. We were so close to where she was that I could see the freckles on her high cheekbones. Her teeth seemed a little larger than normal, as they could be seen slightly through her closed lips, but it didn't take away from her looks. She had on a small crown, necklace, rings, and bracelets, and all were made out of bronze. She literally had on a fortune's worth of bronze, which, when compared to the jewels of Amelia, made Amelia look as poor as I was.

Her dress was green, and flaunted a very low cut in the front. For a woman of almost forty, she didn't look out of her twenties. Empress Selen Nal stood for a moment and waved at the crowd, who in return performed a slight bow all at once. Well, all except for Vida and I.

As she stood, a man walked from the side of the stairs and addressed the crowd in the hall. He was an unusually tall man, with a square-shaped head, long gray hair, and a complexion as red as Ember's shirt. He had on the uniform of a guard, but he also had on a helmet, golden shoulder pads, and a decorated sword on his side. He had rank, whoever he was.

You didn't wear stuff like that if you were a guard who still had to get their hands dirty. No, he likely bossed other soldiers around. Despite that, he was still likely dangerous. Ember had always said to respect guards, but to never underestimate a guard's leader. They earned that position through blood, sweat, and the deaths of others.

"Royal and noble guests!" the man said in a booming voice as he waved his hands around like a showman. "I am pleased to present our Lord, the supreme ruler of The Prime Sovereignty, King of all Kings, Vanquisher of armies, and the resurrected Immortal, chosen by The Keeper." He was really starting to make me see how this job was going to be complicated.

"Emperor Anavor Nal," the man announced as the people in the hall erupted with clapping and shouts.

I glanced at our table and saw Rema. She clapped her hands slightly, but I couldn't help but notice her eyes rolling. I began clapping as well, and soon so did Vida and Ember. Jolin, however, didn't. He simply looked to the front, where the Emperor made his entrance.

For an immortal, the Emperor didn't look very intimidating. Then again, when you couldn't die, why would you need to? He, for all intents and purposes, looked like a normal man. I was unsure how old he was, because, after the first resurrection, he had begun to age more slowly. He had olive-colored skin that had a stretched appearance to it. As if he had too much face to cover, and was running out of skin. His hair was short and blond, and his face was mostly smooth, except for some hair on his chin, and a few warts on his left cheek. He wasn't as tall as Remy or as muscular as Ember. He was just—average.

His pants seemed to be the normal clothing of a royal, and his shirt seemed to be made out of leather, much like our greaves and bracers. He had a sword attached to his side, the same sword it was said had been in his hand the first time he had died.

The Emperor had died six times since then. Was it six? I thought it was six, but it could have been more. It was hard to keep up with such things. He was also the first person to ever display this power. Warpers were known. Apparently even Tongues and Changelings were know. But never had there been an immortal before.

The Emperor waved and then motioned for us all to sit.

There wasn't a grand speech, as I had expected, or anything that came even close to the Emperor acknowledging us. After we sat down, the hall music started, and everything continued as normal. Food was placed before the Emperor and his wife, and, just like most of the people in the hall, they ate, drank, and spoke to those who had enough ranking to go and speak to them. Rema herself had spoken to them, with Ember by her side, for a few minutes.

Once we were all back at the table, the large man who made introductions for the Emperor finally made his way over.

"Rema, I hear you have a very well-known guest with you this evening. Well-known, but I have never heard of him," the man said.

Jolin eyed me quickly with a look on his face that said, *we've been found out. Run!*

Rema simply smiled at the remarks. "I wouldn't say well known, Dutch,, but when you have as much wealth as Clips, you can afford to be out of the public eye while others work for you."

Rema turned and smiled at Ember. "Isn't that right, dear?"

Ember put down his eighth glass of wine and smiled. "Indeed," he said, and then motioned for more wine to be brought over.

As this Dutch gentleman took us all in, Rema gave Jolin a weird eye, and Jolin casually stepped forward to Dutch.

"Would you say the halls of the palace are pretty empty now?" Jolin said, but this time in the voice of a Tongue. The effect wasn't as noticeable this time. Maybe because I wasn't as close to him, or in his direct line of sight, but I could feel that hint of bliss and harmony in the air.

I had been instructed to try to stay to the distant side of Jolin when he used his abilities, to not feel the full effect, and I'm glad I listened. I didn't like being so out of control, and, according to Ember, if you were subject to a Tongue's voice for too long, the effects on your brain would be less than enjoyable.

"Yes, everyone has been relocated to the hall. Even some of the palace guard," Dutch said as he looked blankly into space. Jolin stepped back, and before Dutch could question why he had been asked such a thing, Rema stood up and offered her arm to him for a dance.

Dutch shook his head some. He clearly wasn't a person

who was experienced in being questioned by a Tongue. He placed his arm in Rema's and led her to the dance floor.

"Looks like it's now or never, you two," Ember said as he continued to drink.

Vida and I got up from the table and made our way near the back of the ball, and slipped out into the unattended halls. Now all we had to do was search an entire palace for secrets.

14

We quickly moved away from the hall where the ball was being held. In what seemed like no time, we had made enough turns that we couldn't even hear the music playing anymore. Each hall corridor looked almost the same. Long, dimly lit with lamps, paintings on the wall, and more windows than I had ever seen in one place before.

Without realizing it, I found myself following Vida as she navigated through the corridors.

"Will you slow down for a second?" I hissed. "Shouldn't we look around or something? At least figure out where we are going before we get lost and can't find our way back?"

"Don't tell me the Warper is scared," Vida said with a smirk.

I stiffened some. "Of course I'm not scared. Any of these windows could be my way out. All I need to do is see. I'm more worried about you."

I paused as the words left my mouth. Maybe it didn't sound as bad as I thought, but judging from how she was looking at me, saying I was worried about her had caught her off guard, too. "What I mean is—"

She held her hand up to silence me. We stood in a corridor, and at the other end, coming from a joining corridor, we saw a shadow moving against the wall by a lamp's light.

The shadow grew in size on the wall as it continued to move in our direction. Quickly, I warped back down the hall the way we had come, and hid in a dark corner. Vida followed and joined me, but, naturally she was much slower. We hid in the dark corner of a door opening and waited. The footsteps were clearer now.

A person finally came around the corner. I got low and peeked out from where we were hidden. It was a guard. Or I thought it was a guard. The clothing was different.

"What are you doing?" Vida whispered to me as I continued to peek my eye around the corner.

"Trying to see what that thing is," I said back to her.

"What you're trying to do is get us executed."

I ignored her as she hugged the wall. I stuck my head out a little more to watch it walk up the corridor towards us.

Slowly, I rose and stood tall so as to get a better view of the guard. It was a man. A very large and solid man, dressed in all black from head to toe. I couldn't see a single bit of skin on him. As the man continued to walk towards us, I could see that, where his face should have been, there was a mask. A masked carved like some sort of animal, and where the eyes were was merely a purple glow.

At his side was a long sword made out of some black metal that I could only assume was steel. The man went to turn down another hall, but then stopped. His hand went to his sword handle and he quickly spun and looked in my direction. Instinct took over, and I jumped into the dark corner and pressed myself against the wall.

At least, I intended to press myself against the wall. What I had done was press myself against the body of Vida. My knees got weak; I simply refused to move until I could hear the man walk away. Her body was warm as I pressed against her, and she looked up at me with a mixture of laughter and anger on her face.

My heart skipped when I heard the guard's footsteps began to move in a different direction again. Vida pushed me off her.

"Did you get a good look at whatever you think you saw?"

I stammered as I shook my head. "Uh, yeah. I just don't know what it was," I said as I slowly stepped out in the corridor.

"No need to wait for it to come back again," Vida said as she stepped out into the corridor.

In that brief moment between when I stepped out into the corridor and turned to her, she had changed her clothing. Instead of her dress, she was now wearing a pair of tight trousers, a shirt, and a cloak. I was jealous, because seeing this made me miss my cloak. Not to mention she looked more comfortable than I was in my formal attire.

"I know where the Emperor's quarters are. We should check there first," she said as she dashed down the hall. Even though she was moving with almost full speed, she didn't make a sound.

I warped behind her and appeared beside her as she reached the end of the hall. "You know where the Emperor's quarters are? Why are you just now saying something about it?" I asked her as we kept moving.

"I couldn't tell Rema I knew, otherwise she'd assume it would be easy and try to pay me less. If she thought I had to use my skills as a spy, and find it the hard way, I'd get paid more," she said as she hugged the wall and caught her breath. She made a good point. "It should be close, if I'm remembering correctly. It was a few years ago, so I'm kind of going with the flow. Keeper be with me," she said as she dashed down the hall again.

Going with the flow didn't sit well with me. For all I

knew, we could be flowing in the wrong direction, and this ball in the palace couldn't last forever. Eventually the corridors would be full again.

With every turn we made around a corner, we paused and inspected it slowly, just in case that guard came back. I didn't know what he was, but he scared me. I was ashamed to admit it, but those glowing eyes were something I couldn't grasp and didn't want to see again until I had had a chance to talk to Ember about it.

"Okay, wait," Vida said as she placed her hand on my chest. She was against the wall again and I stood there, confused.

"What?" I asked.

She leaned around the corner slightly, and then looked back at me. "The entrance is just up there."

I moved around her slowly and looked around the corner. I could see the entrance. It was a massive black door that stretched almost eight feet tall. Both its sides could open and move freely, and it would make a lot of noise when opened. This wouldn't have been a problem if it wasn't for the three guards standing in front of that very door.

They were not guards like the one I had seen roaming the corridor earlier, but they were guards all the same. All of them carried spears. No swords. In this case, a sword would have been a bad thing in such close quarters. I could warp to the guards and try to defeat them. The spears wouldn't be as effective up close.

Vida, on the other hand, couldn't warp, and those spears would take her down from this distance with no problem.

"Wait here," I whispered. "I'll warp to them, and—"

Before I could finish I felt my stomach turn. Vida's face

had begun to change.

That smooth brown skin and round lips suddenly became replaced with a thick black beard and eyes that were wide and brown. Long black hair shot down her head as she grew several feet. Her tight trousers transformed into the same guard's uniform the three men at the door were wearing. The only thing she was missing was a weapon.

"You need a weapon," I said, looking at the man who had been Vida up and down.

"I can't make a weapon," she said to me in a low deep voice.

"Why not?"

"I don't know. We just can't."

"You can make clothes, but not a weapon? What sense does that make?" I hissed.

"I didn't make the rules, Lox. Ask the Keeper if you ever see him," she growled at me. "Besides, I don't need a weapon. Just wait here."

She cleared her throat and stepped into the corridor, directly in view of the three waiting guards. She had the look, the walk, and even the size. I kept close to the wall and peeked around the corner.

"Hail, Emperor Nal," she said as she walked towards them. She was about fifteen feet away now. Still not close enough. Did guards say stuff like that? I wouldn't think so, but maybe she had heard it before. The three guards looked at each other, and then back to Vida. From the raised brows on them all, I was willing to bet they didn't address each other like that.

"What are you doing here, Bren?" the middle guard said as he watched Vida get closer. She was ten feet away from them now. "It's not time for shifts to change." He was a short man. By far the shortest of the three. He had dark skin and eyes that seemed to pop out of his head as he spoke.

She was two feet away now, and the middle guard touched his spear to Vida's manly chest.

"Move along, Bren," he said. "Now."

"I can't, my friend. I have to get inside that door." The voice that came out was Vida's this time, and not Bren's. It happened so fast that I had to step out from behind the wall to watch it all unfold.

Vida raised the hand that was closest to the spear, and grabbed it just below the blade, spun around, and, using her own speed and momentum, broke the spear in half.

"Bren?" the other guard called out, but Vida was still moving.

Now, holding the broken spear tip in her hand, she used it—not as a blade, but as an extension of herself. The lead guard attacked with what remaining spear he had, using it like a club. Vida crouched low; at the same time she blocked the lead guard's blow with her spear in hand and followed up with a punch to the man's stomach that took his breath away.

I could literally hear the air escape him as his eyes bulged and he leaned over. He was only there for a second, because, as soon as he leaned over, the still-crouching Vida came up with force and delivered a punch to the man's jaw that sent him stumbling to the left. He only stumbled for a foot or so before Vida hit him yet again, this time under the chin, sending him flipping backwards.

This Bren was massive and freakishly strong. When Vida changed into a person, she must have kept their physical attributes. She was strong in her own right, but not strong enough to send a man flying back with one punch.

The second guard was on the move now. For some reason, the third guard, they one who knew Bren, still moved slowly towards his supposed friend. The second guard was faster than Bren and delivered a series of punches and kicks that all connected. Two in Vida's face, one in the chest, and a kick to the side of the leg that made her drop to a knee. This guard was smart enough not to use his spear so close, but he wasn't smart enough to stay at a distance himself.

As he came in to give Vida a finishing blow, she dodged it, and used the wooden end of her broken spear portion to hit the man in the neck with it as she caught the hand coming at her. The guard grabbed his neck for air, and before Vida could attack, the last guard finally swung his spear.

She could see the swing coming well enough to step to the side, forcing the guard to stumble in place. She lunged forward while spinning and delivered an elbow to the back of the guard's head that made him fall and drop his spear.

The faster guard attacked again with punches and kicks that Vida couldn't seem to counter well. As a result, she turned and ran—up the wall.

Once halfway up the wall, she used it for momentum, pushed herself off, and came crashing down on the guard himself with the full weight of the mighty Bren.

Once on the ground, Vida delivered a few strong blows to the guard's face, and he was no more. She slowly stood up and looked around at the three fallen guards. All were still alive and groaning in pain, holding the parts of their bodies that hurt the most.

I moved down the hall to join her. "Let me guess," I asked. "Years of experience?"

She smiled at me. This wasn't a grin, or a nod, but a full-blown smile, and it set my insides on fire and made me hollow all at once.

"Come on," she said as she moved to the massive double door.

"Bren." The voice surprised us. It was the fallen guard, still on the ground with his hand stretched out. "How could you, Bren? We went to the academy together."

Vida released the door handle as she turned to face the fallen guard.

She kicked him in the face, and his head hit the floor again. In an instant, she changed from the hulking form of Bren, into her normal appearance.

"The door is locked," she said as she came towards me.

"Maybe they have a key," I replied, looking down on the fallen guards. We searched all three men, and, aside from a few gold yolars that Vida kept, we found no keys. I tried to pull on the door, but nothing happened.

"We may have a way in," I said as I dropped down on my knee.

"What are you doing?" Vida asked as she leaned over, looking with me.

"It's a key hole," I said as I looked at her. She gave me a blank expression in return. Luckily, it was large enough for me to see through, and there was a lamp burning on the other side. Perfect line of sight.

"Wait here," I said to her, without looking up.

Through this keyhole doorway, I warped inside.

15

I reappeared on the opposite side of the door and looked around. Once, I would have been too afraid to do what I had just done. For some reason, I use to imagine getting stuck inside of places I used to warp. Cracks in a wall, for example. Now I knew any place was possible as long as I could see where I was going.

I heard a faint knock on the other side of the door.

"Come on, Warps," Vida's voiced sounded from the other side.

I opened it slightly to allow her to walk in.

"Warps?" I asked her.

She walked past me and patted my stomach lightly. "You. I think that sounds better than saying Lox all the time."

I stood and watched her walk away a little longer than I intended before I warped a few feet to catch up with her.

As we left the door behind us, we realized what we had thought to be the entry into the Emperor's room was actually the entrance to two.

"That's strange," Vida said as she looked inside the room on the left, and then peered into the room on the right.

"We're running out of time," I said as I looked inside the room on the right. It smelled faintly sweet, like perfume. This room must have belonged to Empress Selen. It was odd that they were sleeping in two completely different rooms.

"I'll check over here, and you take that one," I said to her as I pointed her towards the emperor's quarters.

On Selen's side, the room was enormous. I felt like a house could fit in this room alone. The windows seemed to stretch as much as ten feet high and gave a perfect view of surrounding Thera. Her bed alone could have held five people with ease, and so could the wardrobe where her clothes were kept. Her entire room was clean, but had signs of use..

The only area in the room that seemed out of order was a large desk in the corner, facing out of a window. I warped to it quickly. Even this desk was larger than life. Indeed, I had seen beds smaller than this desk. I sat down in the chair and began to go through all of her drawers and inspected everything I came in contact with. I was beginning to think it was pointless—until I came across a single envelope with a seal on it.

It wasn't the emperor's seal, but it favored it. It was the seal of the High Lady, Empress Selen Nal's mother.

"Well, this could be useful," I said under my breath as I opened the letter. In my mind I doubted any use would come from it at all, but our time was running out, and we had accomplished nothing so far. At the same time I heard footsteps coming from the other side.

"He keeps an oddly clean room for a man, Emperor or not.," Vida said as she entered. "Almost as if he doesn't even use the room."

That was odd. If the Emperor didn't use his room, where did he sleep? Maybe he had a mistress, as so many of the royals and nobles did.

"Look at this," I said as Vida came up behind me and looked over my shoulder. She came so close to me to see the letter that I could feel her hair against my face. I read the letter out loud:

Dearest Selen,

Daughter, I fear that you are losing yourself in this game you continue to play. The Keeper watches over you. He has blessed you, and you use your gifts for such pointless ends. I fear the daughter I raised has become a person I hardly even know. We enjoy the wealth, privilege, and respect that comes with your union, but I don't even know who you are married to anymore. The deaths. The murders. The lies. The secrets. All for power. The Keeper is watching, and always does. Please, I beg of you, stop this madness while you still can. You are not immortal. None of us are. I know this letter alone will not stay your hand or sway your thoughts, so I will venture from my home to the palace, the day after the ball, to speak with you in person. Until then, my child, I hope you hear my words. I love you so very much, and I still remember who you are.

Love,

The High Lady

Eve Bredon

I closed the letter and put it back where I had found it. "Interesting," I said as I glanced to Vida. She raised her brow.

"Was it?" she asked. She had already headed to the entrance of the room.

"The High Lady clearly knows something. And listen to what she says. She talks about nobody being immortal."

We both looked at each other for a second as the words I said hung in the air.

"She could know how to actually kill the Emperor."

"Why would she know?" Vida asked.

"You know how mothers are. They ask questions. Worry about their kids. I'm certain the High Lady made Selen tell her, at some point, how to stop her husband in case they ever needed to." I felt a fire inside me come to life.

I was certain that the High Lady had answers, but how to get them? That was something for the others to worry about.

"What's wrong?" I asked Vida. She was simply looking at me.

"I don't know."

"Don't know what?" I asked.

"How mothers are." She turned away from me. "Come on, we need to go."

I had forgotten Vida was raised on the streets at such a young age. She hadn't experienced what myself, and clearly Selen, had, a mother always asking questions and wanting us to do the right thing.

"Sorry," I said as I walked behind her. "I didn't think, and—"

"It's okay," she said with a smile. I couldn't tell if she was really okay or not. Vida was so strong and seemed to be able to block things with ease.

We made our way up the small hall and back to the large doors.

"I'm guessing you have a mom like that too, huh, Warps? Like The High Lady. Always worries about you." She had called me *Warps* again. It really was a stupid name, but I didn't say anything about it.

"Yeah I do. A mother that thinks that every time she sees me will be the last, and a younger brother and sister who simply think their older brother can move really fast. I'm all they have," I said as we began to move back down the hall we had come in from. The guards were all still on the ground. Just how hard had Bren hit them?

"Then why do it?" Vida asked as she peered around a corner.

"Why do what?"

"Why risk your life all the time, if you are all they have?"

I followed her around another corner, and we quickly had to duck low behind a table as some guards walked past on an adjoining corridor.

"Because I'm literally all they have," I whispered in her ear. "My jobs, the contracts Ember gets—most of my yolars go to them."

She looked back at me and smiled some. "You're a good guy, Warps. Well, for a killer and all. "Come on, I think we can get back to the main hall before it's over. We should be pretty—what in Keeper's name is that?" Vida said, stopping so abruptly in the corridor that I bumped into her.

We both stood in the corridor, mouths half open as we watched a foot pop inside the corridor—from a window. We were easily six floors up, so how could a foot be coming from outside?

Naturally, the foot was followed by a leg, and then another foot and leg, and finally some hands as a man pulled himself inside of the corridor. A thin man of average height stood before us. He had long, matted black hair that was covered in some sort of scarf and tied at the back. His clothes appeared to be a little too big for him. He had on some worn black trousers, a green shirt, and a leather vest. He was also soaking wet. Why didn't he have on a cloak? It wasn't as if the rain that came every night was new.

We didn't bother to move or hide. If he was coming in this way, he had even less right to be here than we did. We, at least, had come through the front door.

The man stood up and looked down both sides of the corridor. Then he saw us.

He jerked for a minute, and then realized we weren't guards.

"Oh, hey there," he said with an accent as he did a slight bow before us. He then put up a finger to hold us off and he returned back to the window.

I thought he was going back outside until he leaned over and extended his hand. Then, he pulled in another man, who was also soaking wet, and apparently waiting outside, somehow, for him.

"Hello, chaps. Don't you mind us. Plenty in here for us all," he said as he made to move.

I warped in front of him and blocked his way.

"Keeper! A Warper," he said, as he touched his finger to my forehead sternly, as if to see if I was real. "Haven't seen a Warper in ages."

He backed up slowly, towards the window and his companion. He then looked me up and down. "A Warper, minus the cloak and weapons?" he asked. I didn't reply, and he didn't move. "No need to risk it, I suppose."

"What are you doing here?" Vida said as she grabbed the second man who had come through the window by his damp white shirt. She pushed him to the wall hard, but he only smiled at her, and then looked back to the first man. His teeth were so white that they seemed like miniature moons.

The first man held his hands out, as if to keep us at bay as he quickly spoke.

"Let's start over. I'm Craydon. Craydon Addersfield. Man of many talents, but I only use one. Getting into places I shouldn't and taking what I can once inside."

"That sounds like two talents," I said to him.

He looked up into the air as if he were thinking, silently moving his mouth, and raised his brow. "I guess you're right," Craydon said.

Vida slammed Craydon's friend against the wall again.

"Hey, come on now, girlie. Easy," Craydon said. "He don't talk much. Well, he doesn't talk at all, if you want to be honest about it. I call him Rollins." Craydon placed his hand on Rollins' shoulder and tried to get Vida off of him. He failed.

"Why are you and Rollins here?" Vida said as she looked at Craydon, who was still trying to pry her fingers from around Rollins' wet shirt. Rollins, however, just stood there calmly, smiling, and looking at me. He paid no attention to Vida. His gaze felt—odd and familiar all at once.

"I'm here for the same reason as you," Craydon said. "To steal things while the upper class of Thera drink and dance themselves into hibernation."

Vida released Rollins. Craydon stood in front of Rollins and fixed his shirt for him.

"I hit five noble houses solo before I decided to try the palace. Couldn't do it alone, and by the Keeper's luck, I bumped into Rollins here. Literally—I was walking and thinking that I could use some help on this next gig, and we collided into each other. He can't speak, and may not even understand what's going on, but he's an extra pair of hands, and that's all I need," Craydon said as he slapped Rollins on both shoulders.

"You have to leave, now," I said. I didn't care if he had come here to steal things—just not tonight. We needed to keep the element of surprise, and that didn't involve some random thief leaving signs that somebody uninvited was here.

"Leave?" Craydon said as he looked at me. "I'm here to steal, you're here to do what Warpers do, and she—" He looked at Vida, who had a scowl on her face. "She's just scary, to be honest," Craydon said. "We all can get what we want, I'm sure."

"No, we can't," I said to him. "Come back tomorrow, because we can't have signs that people from the outside were here tonight." This wasn't actually a lie, either. So far, Vida and I had covered our tracks well. Even when she had assaulted the guards, they had only seen themselves being attacked by one of their own.

"A Warper, not here to kill, who wants to be stealthy? Curious. Well, we will leave, but it will cost you." Craydon rubbed his chin. "Three silver yolars."

Vida exhaled deeply and balled her fist, and then suddenly turned and looked out the window.

"Warps! People are leaving," she said to me.

I could feel my calm tone fading. This idiot was wasting time we didn't have anymore.

"Okay, I'm done talking. Leave the way you came, or you and Rollins get thrown from this window." Naturally, I couldn't throw him from a window. It would cause the curse to take effect, and draw too much attention. Vida, on the other hand, likely *would* throw them out.

Craydon, grabbing onto Rollins arm, quickly pulled him to the side and away from the window. "I have another idea, Warps," Craydon said.

"Guards! Guards! Help! Intruder! Save the Emperor!" Craydon shouted, over and over again, as his voice echoed through the corridor. Then, with Rollins in tow, he dashed off down the hall in the direction we had come. I had no doubt in my mind that he would end up at the Emperor's quarters.

"That pile of lopeseal," Vida shouted through clenched teeth. "If I ever see him—"

Her words faded away as her mouth hung open, and she slowly stepped back. Whatever she had seen was behind me, on the other end of the corridor. Against my better judgment, I turned and looked, expecting to see guards—but guards wouldn't put that look on Vida's face.

What I did see was the figure of a woman. A woman dressed in all black from head to toe, holding a massive double-sided axe. She wore the mask of a monster, and in the mask's holes were glowing globes of purple.

The axe cut through the air a few times, and then this thing, this beast of a woman, charged towards us.

16

This woman moved quickly, dragging her axe behind her as she ran, sending sparks flying from the corridor floor. I grabbed the throwing knives that were hidden on me. I only had two, so whatever I did with them, I needed to make it count. Vida placed her feet and balled her fist. I could feel my grip tightening around the handle of my knife.

The woman in black was about ten feet away now. I stepped to the side a little, drew my arm in close, and then let my knife fly. It was a good shot. Full of power and precision that only one trained as a Warper could deliver.

And she blocked it with a swipe of her axe as she ran. She never even slowed down. How was she swinging that huge axe so easily?

I decided to keep my second knife in my hand, in hopes of being able to deliver some damage. As the woman got within arm's distance, she jumped and flipped over us with ease. Silently, she landed and spun, kicking Vida in the face and sending her to the ground. Her axe swung at me, and I dodged it as I heard a loud bang against the stone corridor wall.

Glancing over my shoulder, I could see where the axe had connected with the wall, leaving a massive chunk missing and debris on the floor. I slashed with my knife, but the woman, still holding her axe, caught my attack with her free hand.

She had a grip like nothing I had ever felt before. The pain was instant as she began to squeeze my forearm. I tried to free my hand, sending blow after blow with my knife to her midsection. She only looked at me with those glowing purple eyes.

Her axe-wielding hand came up in the air. She was going to try to chop my arm off.

Vida was back on her feet now, and punched this woman-beast square in the chest. The punch had no effect; the woman looked down, and then gave Vida a backhand to the face. The sound of her hand connecting with Vida's face echoed through the corridor, and blood erupted from Vida's mouth.

The only saving grace of that final attack was my hand. The woman let it go in order to attack Vida, and I used the moment to go on the offense.

I needed to get that axe away from her. She was clearly strong, unnaturally so, and she would be a problem, but at least she wouldn't have an axe the size of my body to swing at me. Vida was back on her feet yet again, but she was moving more slowly than before, and her face was beginning to bruise.

"Let's try this one more time," she hissed as she wiped some blood from her mouth.

She wasn't afraid, I'd give her that.

The axe came at me again, and I jumped back slightly as it sliced through the air near my stomach.

Her massive swing put the lady in black off-balance some. I used his moment to try and get the axe away. With my knife out, I closed in, and struck at certain points that gave the arm strength.

The axe should have fallen. Her arm should have been limp and in pain, but the woman in the mask continued to hold her axe.

"How are you able to—" I began as the woman drew

back her small fist and punched me right in the face. I fell down, and things began to spin and turn slightly black. I could hear Vida attacking as I placed my hand on the ground to try and push myself up.

This woman must have had the strength of five men, because I'd been hit before. Plenty of times, and never had it hurt this badly. We were losing this fight, and making enough noise to shake the walls as we did it. Reinforcements, as if this beast woman needed them, would be here soon, and I could only hope it would be normal guards and not the male beast that I had seen earlier.

Vida screamed as the woman placed her hand around her neck and squeezed, lifting her off the ground with ease, as if she was a child.

"No!" I shouted as I did the only thing I could. I ran at her, using my entire body as a weapon, and threw myself on the woman in black. She fell, and so did Vida. It wasn't pretty, but it worked.

I wrestled with the woman on the ground, trying to keep her contained, but I was failing. My entire body hurt. I felt like I had run full speed into a wall.

"Go!" I yelled at Vida.

She coughed and rubbed her throat. "I'm not leaving you here. We can finish this."

She was mad. I respected her lack of fear and determination, but she was utterly mad. One thing you learned early on as a Warper—you're not invincible, and you have to know when to cut your losses and attack another day. This moment right now was one of those times.

"We can't win this now. Run. Get out of the palace and—"

My words were cut off; I groaned as the woman's fist

found my stomach. The punch seemed to make my world stand still as pain consumed my body and took my breath away. I could feel the woman overpowering me. The punch had done its job.

The little bit of fight I had been putting up was almost gone. I needed Vida to go. The woman grabbed my hand and began to squeeze, bending it away from her at the same time. This wasn't good.

"Vida, go!" I shouted. "Escape through the palace. Once you're clear of this corridor, I'll Warp away from a window. Please." Just talking seemed to be sapping away my energy, but this last part seemed to do the trick. Vida looked at me for a moment, battling herself and her emotions, and then turned and ran as fast as she could down the corridor.

She was out of sight in seconds. She would head to the meeting point. The plan was simple. If Vida and I didn't make it back to the hall before the ball was over, everyone was to consider that something had gone wrong, and we would meet at a secondary safe house in Thera. The Thornes owned a lot of property, it seemed.

Now that she was gone, or at least out of sight, I could get away. I stopped struggling with the woman beast and let go. I couldn't see a face under the mask, and those glowing purple orbs where eyes should have been didn't even move, but I could tell she was surprised, because her head tilted slightly. Her grip on me relaxed some, and then, with strength no normal person could wield, she pushed me single-handedly off of her and sent me flying to the wall.

I felt something crack as I hit the wall and slid down on the floor. I coughed and squeezed my eyes shut as they adjusted. I could taste blood in my mouth now, and my head was throbbing. It felt like it was going to explode. The woman was on her feet now, axe yet again in hand, dragging it mockingly on the ground.

She was waiting. Waiting for me to get up. No—she wasn't waiting, she was playing. She knew I couldn't win, and she seemed like a hunter who wanted to have fun with her prey. Well, I didn't want to play anymore.

I pulled myself up, and as I did so, I looked out one of the corridor's windows. The same one we had seen Craydon climbing in from. I squinted my eyes, and felt a ping of happiness. I was going to be safe. I was going to warp away and live to fight another day. I didn't need a great place to warp; I just needed to get out.

I heard the woman move behind me, in my direction. I picked a large house across the street as my destination.

"Later, you stupid pile of lopeseal," I said out loud to the woman approaching me. The blood I tasted in my mouth, and the pain all over my body, told me I needed to insult this beast, just once, before I warped away.

I looked at the building one more time, reached inside myself for that forbidden power, and warped.

Or at least I tried to.

"What?" I said as I looked down at myself. I didn't warp. I tried again and again, but I didn't warp. I couldn't warp. That portion of greatness, that power inside me—I couldn't feel it anymore. It wasn't there.

The woman beast stopped moving, and let out a sound that made my hair stand on end. A low, rumbling, muffled sound. She was laughing. Laughing at me. She knew what was happening. She drew her axe, and came towards me.

I didn't have many options. Actually, I didn't have any options. It wasn't ideal, but it was the only choice I had. I leaped out the window and began my descent towards the ground, and likely my death.

17

Falling to your death is a unique experience. Even though the window I had leapt from was only about six stories up, my fall seemed to take longer than it should have. As if I was moving in slow motion. As I fell I felt—angry.

I had allowed things get out of hand all too fast. Then I thought about it some more, and realized it hadn't been me at all. It had been that Craydon guy. He had alerted the guards—he had brought one of those things down on us that almost got me killed. Not only me, but Vida, too. Had she made it out?

I could only hope so, because, as I fell through the skyline of Thera, I realized I might never see her again. We seemed to have been getting along so well, and now I'd never know if it could have been more, like I desperately wanted.

This wasn't me. I didn't give up. I wasn't raised that way, and I wasn't trained that way. This wasn't going to be how my story ended.

I continued to fall through the sky. Now that my moment of realization had come, that this wasn't the end for me, it seemed to also make time pass normally. I stretched my hand out to my left, hoping against hope that I could grab something, anything to help slow my fall.

I was too far from the palace walls, and my arms weren't able to reach. Why couldn't I warp? I spun around in the air as the ground came closer. I could barely see around me now, because the rain had started to fall hard, making everything seem gray. I spread my arms wide, trying to slow my fall.

I couldn't think like that. I needed to warp. I needed to try. I had fallen so far now that I couldn't afford to be picky on my location. I just needed to be anywhere else. I was coming up on a small shack-like building near the palace. It was a small target, but it was all I had.

I narrowed my eyes on the approaching building as I fell. I reached inside of myself, hoping for it to be there. I was scared, and I was desperate. Almost to the point that I even would have asked The Keeper for help, but I didn't. I still had hope.

I reached inside myself for that portion of the unknown that had allowed me to warp. Nothing was there. I kept trying and trying as I fell. Nothing was there. Nothing was there. The shack was close now, and so was the ground. I reached inside of myself once more, perhaps for the final time.

Power.

Power was there now! Stronger than it had ever been. Raw, untapped, reborn power. I took hold of that power inside of myself, feeling it flow through my body inside and out. I was alive again, it was alive again, and I warped.

I found my target and landed on the roof of the building, but because my warp, something I usually did with little momentum, was powered by my fall, it actually sent me through the roof and inside the store. The noise was loud, and I'm sure the people surrounding could hear it.

I simply laid there for a second on my back, bleeding and in pain. The rain fell through the newly-created hole in the roof and landed on my face. It felt good. Like tiny drops of realization, slapping me. I needed to get moving.

I pulled myself up and looked around the store.

"I don't care what it is. Take that door down and get inside," a voice came back. It was the voice of a man, and he wasn't frantic at all. He was stern and forceful. "There were intruders in the palace corridors tonight, and this may be one of them. We were told they were injured, but still, approach with caution. Now get in there," the man shouted.

His scream wasn't answered by salutes or people agreeing with him; they were answered by action. Footsteps rushed to the building. The front door began to shake and rattle as it was attacked. Even the walls moved. It seemed like they were coming from all sides. I saw a window—a small window. Had it been larger, and closer to the ground, I'm sure they would have tried to come in through it.

This window was enough for me to see out of, and that would be my way out. I moved across the small shop.

The window was closer to the ceiling than I had thought. I actually had to stand on the tips of my toes to see out of it. It was at this moment that I noticed two things. The first was that there seemed to be feet on the roof now. They were smarter than I had expected, and had decided to just come in the same way I had. They would be inside and on me in moments.

The second thing I noticed was that I knew the man giving the orders. He was tall, had long gray hair, a square shaped head, and skin that had a reddish hue to it. "Dutch," I said to myself. The same man who had introduced the Emperor at the ball.

A loud thud sounded off behind me. Then another and another.

"Turn around slowly," a voice behind me said. I could only assume it was a guard, because I couldn't turn around. No—I had to keep looking out this window. It was my only way out. Thankfully, between the darkness inside, and the rain falling in, the guards couldn't see my face.

I looked out the window once more and warped away, leaving the guards and Dutch himself behind.

18

"They're called Battle Born," Ember said as he stood in front of us all. I had finally made it to the second safe house, and it was oddly similar to the first, just on a smaller scale. Unusually clean, and rarely used. We were also further out from the palace now, but still inside the borders of Thera.

Vida had made it back long before I had, and had told the others what we'd found and what had happened. She'd even told them about Craydon Addersfield. A name that none, not even Ember, had heard of.

This time we all sat in chairs, except for Jolin, who was sprawled out on the floor, on his back, beside Sprits, and Ember, who stood in the center, talking.

I sat in a chair across from Vida, while Rema and Remy shared a seat on the sofa.

"Some people," Ember continued, "don't even think they exist. Most people who see them don't live to speak about it, but others, myself included, know better." He stood before the fireplace, looking into it. The room was silent as he paused, and the crackle from the fireplace almost seemed amplified in our silence.

"I don't know what they are, but normal isn't it," Vida said. "Warps and I had a time just getting away from that one. No matter what we threw at her, she kept coming."

"That's because you faced a female," Ember said as he glanced over at Vida. "

According to rumors, with Battle Born, the roles are reversed. The women are smaller, but wield immense strength, and a tolerance for pain that's unmatched, but they are slower. The men, however, wield speed. Able to move and react on an unparalleled level. I fought a male, and even if I had been able to warp, it would have been hard to escape it."

I could feel my eyes bulge a little at this part. "You couldn't warp either?" I asked. I hadn't told them this part yet. I had wanted to wait and tell Ember in private.

Ember shook his head. "No. It's the eyes."

"The eyes?" Jolin asked.

Ember shook his head. "The Battle Born have these glowing purple eyes. What else is under that monstrous mask is unknown, but those eyes, according to what is whispered, at least, can halt a person's Keeper-given abilities."

Those eyes. I felt like I was going to see them in my dreams for the next few days. At least I knew why I couldn't warp now.

"Had Vida tried to change into a stronger form, like this Bren, she would have found herself unable to. Just as you couldn't warp, Lox."

"I was too busy getting kicked in the head to consider changing," Vida said as she rubbed her still bruised face.

Remy placed the book he had in his hand on his lap. "I have heard about them, too. Well, I've read about them here and there. From all accounts, they seemed to have appeared after the Emperor resurrected the first time. Many accounts claim that these Battle Born were the reason Thera won the war in the first place."

"Where do they come from?" I asked. The room was silent as Ember looked to Remy with his brow raised. Remy, in return, simply shrugged his shoulders.

"We shouldn't worry about them right now," Ember

said.

"We shouldn't?" I asked as I glanced at Vida.

"I agree with Ember," Rema said. She had been so quiet this entire time that I had forgotten about her. She lounged beside her brother, sitting far back in the couch with her legs crossed. "We need to focus our attention on the High Lady."

I perked up at this. With everything that had happened, I had forgotten that The High Lady was coming to the palace.

"It's clear that she knows something," Rema said to the room. "We just have to get her to tell us." She looked at Jolin on the floor.

As her eyes shifted to him, so did every other pair of eyes in the room. Jolin froze for a second and then sat upright on the floor with a sigh.

"What would you have me do, Ms. Rema?" He asked as if he knew what was coming.

"I simply want you to work your magic on The High Lady." As she said this, she had a smile on her face. It wasn't a comforting smile. It actually made my skin shiver, and I wasn't sure why.

"I feel like that is going to be harder than expected," I said to her.

"I have a plan," she said as she stood from the couch. I wasn't surprised at all. As I watched her walk around the room, Rema radiated a superior demeanor. She was so confident and smart. That, combined with her high noble status, made her a formidable foe and a powerful ally. I was just glad that she was on our side.

In many ways, she reminded me of Ember. Deadly in her own unique way, often underestimated, and proven time and time again to be efficient.

"From the letter Lox and Vida found, we know The High Lady will be coming to the palace tomorrow. Considering her age, and where she lives in Thera, she will likely prefer to travel in snowfall, as opposed to rain," Rema said.

"Where she lives?" I asked. This caused Rema to stop and look directly at me. "You know where The High Lady lives?"

"Of course we do," Remy said with a snort. "We're high nobles. Rema and I have both been to The High Lady's home numerous times for one thing or another.

"Trust me, Lox, it's not as fun as it seems. If I could trade places with you, any of you, I would do it in a heartbeat.

"Now, don't get me wrong," he said, as he noticed the glares on him. "Being a high noble has its perks, but it also has its drawbacks. There is almost no freedom. Your entire life is predetermined for you, even who you will marry, if need be. You have the power and wealth to change the lives of many, if you wanted, but can't without approval from the Emperor or royals, both of whom would never allow it, simply to keep the rich in power."

Remy looked down from us all and rubbed his nose with the back of his thumb, and then looked to his sister. "There is a reason she is such a good leader in this family. Because everything about our lives that I despise, she embraces. My dear sister was made for this." He turned away from her and clasped his hands tightly on the book in his lap. "I simply prefer to escape in my books. It's the closest I can get to living another life, or learning about something other than what is expected of me."

Ember had a grimace on his face as he glanced at me. The glares that Vida and Jolin were giving Remy had faded away. Maybe they, like me, almost felt bad for him. I was beginning to see Remy in a different light now. Just as I was born into a life destined to be drenched in blood, so was he as the role of a high noble. I had never considered it could have been a burden.

"That was a very nice speech, Remy," Rema said as she displayed a huge smile on her face. "That's also why your role in this is to simply do nothing."

Remy stood from the couch and walked off. I wasn't sure where he went, but he didn't come back.

"Now, as my brother was saying before all of that pointlessness, we know where The High Lady calls home. In the morning, I want you—"She pointed to Jolin—"to go give her a visit before the carriage comes to escort her to the palace, and find out as much as you can about what she knows."

Jolin didn't speak; he simply nodded his head and returned to laying down on the ground.

"I should go with him," Ember said.

Rema shook her head. "No. I need you to stay and reach out to as many of your contacts as you can to see what, if anything, is happening around the Kingdoms. I need to know if any other people are disappearing, or if any other royal families have been told about these people from beyond the waters. Stay your blade for now, and simply gather information. This, naturally, would be better for a spy or a Tongue, but you, as a Warper, will cover more ground in a short time."

Rema looked at me with that dead smile again. "Lox will be our Warper in your absence."

Ember looked at me as he adjusted his cloak and put his hood up. "I need to grab some things from my place before I go. I'll get a few hours of sleep and then I'll be on my way."

He walked to where I sat, placed a firm hand on my shoulder, and leaned over to whisper in my ear.

"Be careful, protect yourself and stay aware. I have a feeling things are about to get complicated."

Rema's head twitched some. "Everything okay?" she asked as she watched Ember speak to me.

"Fine," he said. He walked to a window, and then warped away.

My eyes lingered on the spot where he had stood for a few moments. Ember had a funny feeling about what was to come next, and he was usually right about that sort of thing. Now I was beginning to feel it, too. The team, united as we were, was split up now. Remy was no longer here; Ember had been sent around the five Kingdoms; all that remained were me, Vida, and Jolin. On top of us all was Rema, pulling our strings.

I trusted my instincts, and decided to keep a close eye on both Rema and Remy until Ember returned.

"I suggest you three get some food if you want, and then some sleep. You're going to pay The High Lady a visit at first snowfall." She picked up a lamp, leaving only one burning in the room. "Goodnight, and Keeper be with you tomorrow. I'll see you in the morning to go over the plans before you leave."

She turned and walked away, holding the lamp with her as she moved.

"Mr. Lox, Ms. Vida," Jolin said, with a little nod, as he moved from the floor to the couch. "Tomorrow you get to see me in action, it seems." He stretched out on the couch, put his back to us, and said no more.

"You okay?" I asked Vida. Every time I looked at her bruised face, I felt bad.

"I'll be fine, Warps," she said in a faint smile. "Let's get some food, and then some rest."

She got up and made her way to the kitchen. I watched her walk away from the dim room and vanish into the darkness. I stood up and followed her. I wasn't hungry, but something told me I would need my strength for the morning.

19

I woke up the next morning, seemingly alone. Natural light from outside poured into the room, touching every corner. I peered out the window from the couch I was on and could see the snow falling. As usual, the mixture of snow and sunlight was beautiful.

I was the only person in the room, though. Jolin was gone from the couch he had been sleeping on, and Vida had disappeared from the long chair she had called her resting place the night before.

"Where is everybody?" I said to myself. Instinct took over, and I grabbed my dagger.

Better safe than sorry. As I placed my feet on the ground, I kicked something that yelped. "Sorry, Sprits," I said.

I stood for a moment and simply listened. I could hear voices in the house. Faint voices, but voices nonetheless. I warped a few feet down the hall towards the voices. Warping in these situations were better than simply walking. A creaking floor could be the death of you sometimes.

"Where is everyone?" I heard a voice say as I got closer. It was Rema. I warped a couple of feet closer, reappearing to the side of a cracked door. Judging from what little I could see, this room was designated for Remy. It had a large shelf with a mountain of books on it, a massive bed with posts standing six feet tall, and a table with food sprawled over it.

"Jolin and Vida are preparing outside. They woke up

earlier than expected," Remy replied. I could see Rema walking now. She was dressed in brown trousers and a tight shirt. She went around the table that Remy sat at and allowed her finger to move along the spines of the books.

"And the Warper?" she asked.

I didn't like the way she was talking. As if she didn't want to use our names. Remy looked up from his plate of food. A plate of food that he hadn't touched much of, from what I could see through the crack in the door.

"He's still sleeping on the couch," he replied, as he drank some wine from a larger than normal cup.

"It's a little early for drink, isn't it, Remy?" she said as she eyed her brother, who seemed to be pouring more in the cup. I couldn't actually see what he was doing, but I saw his elbow rise and could hear the sound of falling liquid.

"I don't understand how you are alright with this," Remy said. "They trust us. They have always trusted us, and you want to betray them."

Rema said nothing as she stood tall, with her chest out and chin high. She walked over to the bed, taking wide steps as she did so, and sat on its end. She didn't respond with words. Instead, she gave him a playful grin and a wink. Almost as if she were taunting him.

"All for what?" he continued. "Things we already have. Riches and power."

I couldn't believe what I was hearing. Remy had seemed like the smart one. The one I liked the most, especially after last night. Now he was here, upset that his sister planned to have the Emperor, and likely his wife, killed. How could he feel like she was betraying them, knowing what the Emperor had done?

"Brother, you knew what this was from the start. You also knew what would come of it. If you don't have the stomach for it, then return to the main house, read your books, and act like you knew of nothing. With or without you, the plan will continue."

Remy slammed his hand down on the table, causing his wine to fall over and his plate of food to jump.

"Fine. Fine. I'll return to the main house by today's end. I just hope you know what will come of this," he said. He stood up so forcefully that the chair he was sitting in went flying back. "Let's just hope The Keeper has mercy on you for sending people to their deaths."

"Let's," Rema replied.

I heard a creak on the floor that sounded close to the door I was listening at. Quickly I turned my head and saw the room I had been sleeping in down the hall. I locked my eyes on the couch and warped. Seconds after I reappeared, the door to Remy's room opened and he stormed out. Rema followed behind him. She turned and saw me sitting up on the couch.

I rubbed the back of my neck and wiped my eyes, trying to seem as much like a person who had just woken up as possible.

"Good morning, Mr. Lox," she said as she walked over to me.

"You sound like Jolin now," I said as I cleared my throat.

"Would you prefer if I called you Warps?" she asked, behind a smile.

"No. Just Lox is fine."

I stood up and stretched.

"Where is everyone?" I asked, trying to avoid her eye. I felt that if they lingered too long she would somehow know I heard their conversation.

"Jolin and Vida are outside getting the carriage ready.

My brother is—" She let her words fall short as she looked towards the ground blankly. "He is returning to the main house. Seems all of this is too much for him to handle."

I nodded slightly.

We stood in silence for a second.

"Well, let us get started. Meet us outside when you are ready, but be mindful. We don't have a lot of time."

With those words, she did a slight nod and walked away, heading outside to speak with Jolin and Vida. We didn't actually know what they plan was, and I had a feeling we were about to find out.

Once we were outside, Jolin, Vida, and myself listened to the plan Rema had come up with the night before. She was proving to be as smart as Remy time and time again. It would have taken me a few nights to come up with this plan.

Basically, we needed to get information from The High Lady before her escorts to the palace arrived. What we were to do was simply to serve as a fake escort. Arrive to her home in our fancy carriage provided by the wealth of the Thornes; we were to have Vida change into Bren again, while Jolin would be dressed as the driver. Once there, he would ask her anything he needed to, in order to get answers. At her old age, she should apparently be more vulnerable to his powers as a Tongue. At least, that's what Jolin had said. I was still learning about it as I went.

Then there was my part. I, too, was to dress up as a guard, and provide backup if needed. Rema all but assured that it wouldn't be needed. The only issue was that Rema wasn't able to provide the outfit for me, and, since I couldn't change my appearance like Vida, I would have to acquire one the old-fashioned way. From a guard. A real, live, breathing, weapon-carrying guard. Which wouldn't be hard. I just had to get one alone.

That was why I was currently warping from rooftop to rooftop, searching for a small patrol of guards, or—even better—a lone guard. I needed to be as fast as possible. The High Lady lived almost near the edges of Thera, so it would take a little while to get there; as I hunted, Vida and Jolin had already started the trip.

It all seemed easy enough. I just didn't have any time to waste.

I didn't know why, but something inside of me was drawing me to the portion of Thera that was known for its brothels. I warped to the rooftop of a two-story building that seemed abandoned. It was funny. Just two streets over was where I had failed in hunting Ashland, and here I was again, in the same area.

My luck was proving to be impressive, because, as soon as I reappeared from my warp, I saw a guard. A lone guard, who appeared to be off-duty, and was heading directly to a brothel. I was so shocked to see the guard, almost waiting for me, that it made me pause. I usually didn't get this lucky, and things didn't come easy. I don't know what had pushed me to check this area, but I was glad I had.

I glanced up to the sky for a moment. "Keeper?" I whispered to myself. Then I shook my head and washed those thoughts away. "Don't be foolish. You had a gut feeling that worked in your favor," I said under my breath.

I felt naked as I crouched here, without my cloak, trying to stay hidden as I watched the guard. I had decided to leave my cloak behind, since I was going to discard my current clothing anyway.

The guard was so set on his destination that he didn't even notice me when I reappeared from a warp, not even a foot behind him. The street was empty. This, too, seemed to play in my favor. The ease of this all set a knot in my stomach. It all seemed too easy. Like the world around me was being bent so that everything worked out.

I came in close to the guard, standing slightly to his left side. The side his sword swung on.

"Excuse me," I said as the guard stopped and turned around.

"Be quick, boy, I—" The guard's words were silenced by my fist to his throat. He placed both hands on his throat and struggled to breathe.

With his hands up on his neck, his stomach was open and unprotected. I had two options here. Punch him in the stomach, or kick him in his stomach. The latter would get the job done faster, and I had a schedule to keep.

I spun around to build momentum and delivered a kick to his stomach. The little air in his body that he had left rushed out in one massive gasp, and he bent over slightly, one hand on his neck and one hand on his stomach. He was exposed, and he was at my mercy.

I could have ended his life. A simple stab or slash of my dagger and he would have taken his last breath as he bled out and died in the street like a rat. It is what Ember would have done. He likely would have made it so the body would have never have been found, too. But if I did that, the curse would start, and I knew how that would end. I took a deep breath, and, instead of ending his life, I opted for extreme pain instead.

As he continued to lean over and try to gather himself, I took a slight push from my foot and sent a knee to the front of his face. As my knee connected, the guard let out a grunt and fell backwards, arms stretched out, on the ground. When he woke, he would have a horrible headache, but he would be alive.

I picked up the body and dragged him to a side alley. He was a little smaller than me, so his clothes were a tight fit in some spots, but I was still able to wear the uniform. I thought about it. The odds of me finding a guard alone, that was nearly my size, were almost impossible. I glanced up to the sky again, and continued to get dressed in silence.

Once fully dressed, I tossed my unneeded clothes and three gold yolars on the guard's body. Still enough for him to enjoy himself at the brothels when he woke up after the pain had passed. That was the least I could do. A small *thank you* from me, as it were. This had been quicker than I expected.

Turning my view to the same building I had been on before I attacked the guard, I warped off in the direction of Jolin and Vida so that I could catch the carriage. I wasn't about to let them have all the fun without me.

20

I caught up to the carriage with ease about ten minutes after I left the guard unconscious in the alley. Warping over buildings was much faster than bending to the rules that came with moving through Thera on foot or by carriage.

I was currently on a taller building now. From my view, it was one of the tallest in the area. Even though I was five stories up, I could see the carriage moving through the city streets. Jolin was taking his role as carriage driver seriously, and was driving with little to no regard for the surroundings.

In the last few seconds alone he had narrowly missed three people walking, two people on bicycles, and he had clipped a building while turning. I shook my head as I warped from the building and reappeared in the street before the oncoming carriage.

Jolin had to pull hard on the reins to bring the caprongs to a halt.

"Mr. Lox!" Jolin shouted as he put a hand to his chest and got his breathing under control. "Are you trying to get run over?" he asked, wiping his forehead with the back of his hand.

"No. But neither is anybody else on the street," I replied. I slowly walked to the side, not taking my eyes off the massive caprongs in front of the carriage. They were such beautiful creatures. Until the horns grew in, that is. Then they were like the caprongs that the guards of Pradeep had ridden.

The thought caused my stomach to churn as I climbed up inside the carriage.

Before I sat down, I stuck my head back outside the carriage.

"Get us there in one piece, please."

Jolin smirked and nodded some as he gave the reigns a good shake once more.

The caprongs flared to life again, unleashing primal sounds while pulling the carriage with ease. We began moving so fast that I was thrown back in my seat, and the door slammed shut beside me.

"You okay there, Warps?" The voice of Vida came from the large manly figure known as Bren, who sat across from me.

"You know, that's just creepy," I said to her. To him. To Vida.

"What is?" she asked.

"Your voice, coming from his body. It's—" I tried to find the a nicer way to say what I was thinking. At that same moment, the face of Bren smiled some and leaned over towards me.

"It's what, Warps?" she said as she rubbed her hand on my thigh. I jumped back in my seat as Vida burst into laughter and tossed her head back.

The face of Bren was turning red now from laughing so hard.

"It's still me, Warps," Vida's voice said through broken laughter.

"Yeah, I know," I replied as I looked out the carriage window. "I'd just rather it be *you* touching me, as yourself."

The words were out of my mouth and into the world of reality before I realized what I said. Had I really just said that?

Her laughter had stopped now, and the only sound was the bumping of the carriage and the occasional screaming person from outside as we passed. I could feel my heart pounding in my chest harder than before.

Bren cleared his throat and stood up from his seat in the carriage. While it was Bren that stood up, it was Vida who sat down beside me. She had changed into herself again. There was plenty of room on the seat, but she had decided to sit close beside me. I felt her hand on my leg again.

"This better?" she said as she looked at me slowly.

All I could think was that she was different. She was her own kind of special, wrapped inside of the right amount of dangerous. She was different, like me, and for some reason that drew me to her.

I had seen her fight, and it was possible that she could have beaten me in a straight-up fight if she wanted to, and that made her even more appealing. I looked at her, sitting beside me now, bobbing up and down as we road in the carriage.

Even now, she was beautiful. The clothes she had on from her recent change were tight just in the right places, causing her curves to stand out. I don't know if this was done on purpose or by accident,and I didn't care.

"It's—"

I opened my mouth to respond, and at that moment she kissed me.

Full force, on the lips, her tongue in my mouth, she kissed me. I had thought that when I warped I was touching greatness, grabbing a lightning bolt, and feeling a sliver of infinity, but this—this kiss was all of those things amplified.

I didn't have much experience in kissing. I went with instinct and pushed back towards her slightly, and she didn't stop. Time was standing still for me, and it was then that I decided to go for an even bigger move. I put my hand on her thigh, and in return, she placed her hand on mine.

I thought she was going to move it, but she didn't. I couldn't feel anything but fire inside of me now. It was as if the carriage had stopped moving, and nothing else existed.

"Hey!" a voice came from outside as it knocked on the carriage door.

We both suddenly stopped kissing. Apparently the carriage really had stopped moving. I looked at Vida, who smiled at me.

"Time to go to work, Warps," she said as her face transformed into Bren's.

The door swung open, and Jolin stood there.

"What are you two doing?" he asked as he saw Bren and I, sitting close and looking at each other.

"Nothing," I said, quickly, as I realized what it must have looked like to him.

Jolin grinned. "Well, hurry up and finish doing nothing. We're here, and we have to hurry."

He left the door open as he left us alone again. I didn't know what to say to her.

"That was—" I searched for the words.

"Your first time?" Vida asked. I didn't reply; I felt heat rushing to my face. "I could tell, but you did good. Plus—" Vida stood to get out of the carriage. "Practice makes perfect."

I could feel my eyes pop open at the realization that more of this was to come.

I stepped out of the carriage and joined Jolin and Vida in front of what seemed to be a larger-than-normal house, behind a gate. I looked to both sides: the gate seemed to surround the entire house and a few small buildings as well. Two men stood in front of the gate, and both had swords at their sides.

These swords were different than ones I had seen on guards before. They seemed more elegant. Instead of a straight blade, they were rounded, like a large hook. Both sides were sharp, and the handle itself had a short blade at the end, too.

"That's smart," I said under my breath to myself. I decided to keep this sword image in my mind as a mental note.

Vida and I stood behind Jolin. Vida, as Bren, was a large and scary man; I myself tried to seem as menacing. I kept my posture straight, and allowed my lips to form a thin line. I looked ahead and tried to act as if this was a normal thing. Now we would see how well Rema's plan would work.

"Good morning, gentlemen. I trust The High Lady has informed you that her escort to the palace would arrive today?" Jolin asked.

The guards stood silent for a second. Then one spoke.

"She did, but you're early. You're not scheduled to arrive for another hour." The guard had a funny accent that I couldn't place. He seemed more nervous than we were, and I could see beads of sweat forming on his forehead, just below his black hair.

Jolin glanced to Bren on his left and then back to the guards. "We left earlier than expected. Now, kindly let us in."

Vida stepped a little closer to the door guard. The guard stepped to the side and removed a large key from his pocket, beginning to unlock the gate.

"Thank you, sir," Jolin said as he walked pass the guard. We followed closely behind him down the walkway.

The area behind the fence, leading up to the house, seemed to be a courtyard. There were various trees that seemed well taken-care-of, sitting areas, and even a tiny fountain. The house itself and the walkway seemed to be made entirely out of stone, something that wasn't commonly done. There hadn't been a previous high lady, and likely wouldn't be a next. The name, the title, and everything associated with it had been created by the Empress for her mother.

Crafting the home entirely out of stone was something done simply to make the place stand out, and it was a success. The fence alone made it stand out. Even the door was unique. Instead of being made out of wood like most doors, it was composed of a mixture of stones, glass, and wood. How they had made it, I'd never know, and to be honest it was a hideous door, but it was different, and apparently that was what the Empress had wanted.

Jolin knocked at the door firmly. "High Lady," he said as he knocked once more. "This should be easy," Jolin said, turning to us. "The older a person, the more vulnerable they are to my abilities."

The door swung open, and there stood a short lady. She was round in the face and body, and slumped over slightly. Like her daughter, she still had red hair, but it was gray in areas. It curled down her head and to her neck slightly.

She smiled, and through the smile her old face seemed to be made bright. Her wrinkles seemed to stand out strong in the light, while her eyes were dim and dull brown. "Come on in," she said as she smiled to us all and walked away.

We followed her into her the house.

While the outside was a marvel to see, inside, the house was pretty normal. Some areas were extremely messy, while others seemed to be cleaned on a daily basis.

"You're early," she said as she walked through the house, using the walls here and there for support. "I was just about to eat." She led us to a room with a large table inside of it.

The table looked as if it could seat over a dozen people, but it had only a few chairs at the end of it.

She sat down and began eating.

"Oh, where are my manners? Would you like some?"

Vida and I stood silent. Guards didn't talk unless addressed directly, and we had to keep up the ruse. In this situation, only Jolin could speak.

The High Lady shoved a chunk of bread in her mouth and chewed it slowly as she sipped a steaming liquid from her cup. Jolin pulled out a seat and sat down beside her.

"Ma'am, Ms. High Lady—is it okay if I ask you some questions as you eat?"

She nodded. "I don't see why you couldn't, my boy," she said as she patted Jolin's hand. I could see him swallow for a second, and he cleared his throat.

Then, it flooded the room, as fast and as bright as sunlight. Stronger than I had ever felt it before. He had done it. Somehow, he had begun to use his ability as a Tongue. He wasn't speaking, but I could feel the effect of it already. It wasn't as strong on me, because I was to the side, but I could feel it in the air. It was as if he could turn it off and on at will before he even started speaking.

Jolin moved his hand from under the hand of The High Lady, and leaned in towards her slightly.

"Can you tell me about the Emperor and you daughter?"

21

The High Lady seemed to enjoy the feeling she got from talking to a Tongue. From the moment Jolin began to use his ability, she had a wide smile on her face. Vida looked at me for a moment and then back to the table where Jolin sat.

"Who were the murdered people you mentioned in the letter you sent the Empress?" Jolin asked as he poured himself some of the hot liquid. I thought it was tea at first, but then noticed it had a yellow tint to it.

"They were selected. They were nothing before my daughter. They were men, they were Emperors," the High Lady responded.

"What does that mean?" Vida said in Bren's deep voice. The High Lady looked at Bren sharply, as if she hadn't noticed us standing there. Jolin, too, glared at Vida, and put his finger up to his lips.

I leaned in and whispered to Jolin. "Find out how we kill the Emperor first. We can get other details later. Killing him is how we get paid."

He nodded his head some as he wiped his eyes with both hands.

"Ms. High Lady," Jolin said, as The High Lady put what seemed to be an extremely long slice of bacon in her mouth and began chewing.

"Emperor Nal. How can he be killed? Do you know?"

Her eyes grew wider as she gasped and looked a Jolin. She didn't respond. I could feel the shift in the air, as if a storm was brewing inside of the house itself. That feeling of bliss and excitement grew as Jolin increased his powers.

"Do you know how to kill the Emperor? Has your daughter ever talked about it to you? What happens when he dies?"

The High Lady began to breathe a little harder than before. In the quiet room her breaths sounded louder than they should have.

"She is the secret to his resurrection," The High Lady said with a snap. What was she talking about? The Empress was the secret to the Emperor's resurrection? That couldn't be right. "He died. He is no immortal. She is the one blessed by the Keeper. Lies! Lies! Lies!" she shouted as she began to shake. "Lies! He is no immortal. He is no Emperor! Not anymore! Lies!"

She screamed over and over as she put her hands to her head.

"Jolin," I said, but he quickly held his hand up to silence me.

"Not now, Mr. Lox. Seems the High Lady is more resistant than I could have imagined."

Something clearly was wrong with The High Lady. She seemed to be in pain from his questions. The feeling in the room had changed again. It continued to grow even stronger than before, and I saw Jolin's eyes becoming red and bloodshot. His was really letting his power flow now, and whatever part of the brain it affected was causing The High Lady to squirm.

"Tell me the truth, High Lady. How is the Empress the secret? How is he not an immortal? He has died and returned time and time again. Tell me."

My head turned quickly as I heard somebody at the front door trying to get in. Vida peeked out of a window. "It's the gate guards," she said.

"Jolin, we need to go," I hissed. "Now."

It was then, through gritted teeth and tears in her eyes, that The High Lady spoke.

"Selen is. Selen is. A Changeling."

I could feel my mouth drop open as I looked to Vida, still standing at the window, whose own mouth gaped open too.

"She changes them. Makes them an Emperor. Puts them in his place. Then they die, and she does it again! Murders! Lies!" She began to scream as blood ran down from her nose.

"Jolin, stop. Stop pushing her!" I screamed.

The door at the front of the house began to shake violently. "What's going on in there?" the guard's voice bellowed as he banged on the door. He sounded more stern than he had when we arrived.

"Not an Immortal! Not an Immortal! They were selected! They were nothing. She is the one blessed by The Keeper." Blood oozed from both of her nostrils now and trickled from her ears as her face grew pale and she fell out of her seat. Dead.

The air in the room, and the unique feeling that came with Jolin's powers, faded away as he looked at Vida and I.

"What happened, Jolin?" Vida asked.

The door continued to shake in the front.

"I—I don't know," Jolin said as he looked at the lifeless body of The High Lady. "Some people handle answering a Tongue differently. The older a person, the weaker they are, and the results can be—" He trailed off without finishing his words.

I looked at her body. Dead. Lifeless, and innocent. I had seen dead bodies before. It was hard to live with Ember for two years and not get used to seeing them. It was a part of the life we lived. The High Lady was different. She had known what her daughter was doing, and wanted to stop it, according to her letter.

Now, because of us, she was dead.

"You heard what she said, didn't you?" Jolin asked as he stood from the table. "It's all a lie. All of it. The Emperor isn't immortal. He can't come back to life at all. Selen, the Empress, is a Changeling, like Vida. She's changing these men and putting them in the Emperor's place."

"We have a bigger problem," Vida said as she looked outside. She was no longer Bren anymore, but her normal self.

I ran to the window she was looking out of. Two new carriages had arrived outside and were coming through the gates. The man banging at the front door had stopped and was approaching the new carriages.

I let out a sigh. "The real escorts for The High Lady are here."

I looked around the room for something, anything, to get us out of this situation. We were vastly outnumbered, and while I was sure that Vida and I could take a few out, Jolin likely would slow us down. He didn't seem much like a fighter. Master of words, perhaps, a secret keeping specialist, but certainly not a fighter.

"Any ideas, Warps?" Vida asked me. "Because I got nothing."

"I, too, am at a loss for ideas, Mr. Lox. This seems to be your realm of expertise," Jolin added.

I walked back and forth for a moment and then looked out the window once more. All of the guard were walking to the house and talking. The one who had stood at the gate earlier seemed to be pointing at the house and telling a story as he moved his hands wildly.

"Four guards from one carriage, five from the other, and the guards from the gate. Eleven guards total." I ran my hands through my hair. I could feel the frustration brewing up inside of me. This was the exact reason Warpers worked alone. If it was just me in here, I could warp away and be done with it, but now I had my burdens. I had my friends.

Vida stood proud beside me, a little closer to me than necessary, and she seemed like she wasn't worried, but her eyes kept darting around, her breathing was faster than normal, and her fists were clenched. She was afraid. Jolin was apparently full of jitters, unable to stop moving, and he had begun to sweat.

"Wait," I said out loud as I took a few steps back. An idea had hit me suddenly that was risky and wild. The window we had been looking out of was big—very big. Big enough for a person to jump out of.

"Vida," I said as I looked at her with a smile.

She jerked her head back slightly. "What?" she asked.

"Change into The High Lady. Jolin, hide the body," I said as I pointed to the woman, dead on the floor.

"Hide the body? Where?" Jolin asked.

"I don't know, anywhere. Just push her under the table or something," I replied.

Jolin began to move quickly. He moved the body some, and then noticed that doing so would leave blood visible on the floor. Instead, he adjusted the body, and simply pushed the table up so that it was now standing over the body.

"Go, now," I said, turning to look at Vida, and jumping back a few feet.

She was no longer Vida—now she was The High Lady. Short, round, and red-haired. She looked up at me.

"Now what?" The voice of Vida came from behind that old face.

"Okay, let the guards in," I began.

"Let them in?" Jolin said. "Mr. Lox—"

"Trust me, Jolin. This will work."

Had I just lied to him to his face? Maybe. It could work, though. It could also fail, but we had few choices. "Let them in, and lead them to this room. I want you both to stay close to this window. When you hear me scream, jump out the window."

Vida and Jolin both looked to the window.

"When you say jump out—" Jolin began.

"Yeah. He means jump *through* the window," Vida finished.

"Only options, guys. You just have to trust me," I said as the guards began again to try the door.

Vida exhaled and rolled her eyes, and began walking slowly and slightly bent, using the wall for support.

Her ability to mimic went far beyond simply changing her appearance. She seemed to have a talent for body language and mannerisms as well. Had I not know it was her, I would have assumed she was the original High Lady.

I looked outside the window, thought to myself, *this is why we work alone*, and then warped outside near the carriages. I reappeared beside the caprongs of the carriages and scared them a little. They began to move and grunt while stomping the ground.

"Easy, easy," I said as I put my hands in the air to get their attention. "It's okay, it's okay."

Quickly, I untied the caprongs tethered to the first carriage. In my head, I expected the caprongs to take off running once set free. But instead they just stood there.

"Go, go. Run free," I said, but they just looked at me. I glanced back at the house, then to the caprongs again. I warped and reappeared in the same spot. This did the trick.

The caprongs attached to the carriage grunted and ran off in different directions, leaving the carriage they had once pulled behind. I did this again for another carriage, before getting to the one we had arrived in.

Now for the next carriage. Instead of releasing these caprongs, I climbed into the driver's seat. Then I sat down and grabbed hold of the reins. I had never been in the driver's seat of a carriage. It felt weird, and I didn't like being this high up. It felt like I could fall off at any moment.

I gently jerked the reins once, forcing the caprongs to move the carriage towards the house. I made sure to stay out of sight so that the guards couldn't see. I positioned the carriage, directly to the side of the window, and positioned the caprongs towards the gate. I hoped Vida and Jolin were okay in there. I took a deep breath and let out a howl that my little brother Luka would have been proud of.

Nothing happened for a moment, and then two bodies exploded from the house. Jolin and The High Lady landed on the ground. Vida landed with grace on her feet, while Jolin tumbled and rolled on the ground. She helped him up quickly, and they jumped on the back of the carriage. We didn't have time for them to get inside. They just held on the handles in the back as I gave a jerk for the caprongs to move.

Speed and energy erupted from the caprongs instantly as we raced down the stone walkway and out through the gates. I could hear screams and curses being hurled at me from the window as we left. Had these guards had spears, we likely wouldn't have made it out alive. Lucky for us, they only had swords.

I raced through the city, not slowing down, and hoping that passersby didn't walk in the way of my high-speed carriage.

"Never insult my driving again, Mr. Lox," Jolin screamed from the back of the carriage as he and Vida held on.

We arrived at the Thornes' home quicker than we'd expected. We were to meet at the larger of the safe-houses in Thera after our conversation with The High Lady. Naturally, at the time of planning, we hadn't expected for her to die in the process. We hadn't been back here since we'd prepared for the ball a night ago. It seemed like so much longer than that. We had been busy.

I got down from the driver's seat and walked to the back. Vida and Jolin were stepping down to the ground. Jolin was bent over, hands on his knees and breathing hard.

"I think I'm going to be sick," he said as he held his stomach.

Vida, who was no longer The High Lady, walked to me with a smile. "That was amazing," she said as she slapped me on the shoulder. It was a good slap. A hard slap, and then she kissed me.

"Oh," Jolin said in surprise.

"Now I know I'm going to be sick."

Secrets, fake immortals, unkillable beasts dressed in black, people disappearing—none of it mattered at this moment. Right now it was just me, Vida, and our—whatever we had for each other. I didn't have a name for it, and I didn't care. No matter what happened next, for this moment, as the snow continued to fall around us, everything was perfect, and nothing mattered.

22

The events that had happened with The High Lady changed everything for us and for our plans. With her death, along with the knowledge of our break-in during the ball, the Empress and Emperor would be on high alert.

They had increased their guards outside the palace and inside as well. Some staff had been replaced, while other staff members had been executed on the spot. In the three days that followed the death of her mother, the Empress soothed her rage with bloodshed, and all of Thera was aware of it

Originally, Ember was to be the one to deliver the final blow to the Emperor after we uncovered the secret to his immortality and his ability to resurrect. But, for reasons unknown, Ember hadn't returned from his time in the other kingdoms. Nobody had heard from him, and even when I tried to feel out where he could be from our bond, I was unable to.

It scared me, and I tried to not think about the idea that he might have been unable to return. I found comfort in knowing that Ember was the best at what he did, and that if he was dead, he didn't go down easy. But why would he be dead? He was only investigating things. Something wasn't right, and I didn't know exactly what it was.

With Ember gone, the responsibility fell to me to be the one to eliminate the Emperor, and now his wife too. She was the one with the power. She was the one finding normal men and changing them into a copy of the Emperor.

That explained why, whenever a resurrection took place, the Emperor didn't appear until days after. He was learning his new role.

So here I was, standing in the rain, under my cloak, dagger and knives in tow, looking at the palace from an adjacent building. A lot was resting on my shoulders, and mine alone. The future of my family depended on this pay day. Jolin and Vida's futures all came to this. Everything that had led up to this moment, as important as it may have been, seemed pointless now.

I gripped my dagger tightly and looked down at it. It suddenly seemed smaller than normal, but there it was. A simple dagger that, for better or worse, was about to change my life. There was no way I walked away from this alive without killing somebody. Then the curse would start, along with my bloody destiny.

I exhaled and placed my dagger in my belt. It was time for part one of a plan that had taken two days to come up with. I jumped off the building and warped as I fell, landing next to one of the smaller buildings near the palace. The street was dark here; the torch runner hadn't made it here yet, but he was coming. I could see him in the distance, igniting the tall lamps in the rain.

A torch runner was exactly what I needed now. I warped closer to the area where I had seen a flame appear on top of the lamp. I reappeared beside him, cloak down and fist balled.

"Keeper," the Torch Runner said in surprise. "You're a—"

I grabbed the man by his cloak and pulled him in close, delivering a fist to his nose and then, in rapid succession, another fist to his throat. I placed my hand on his neck and, with as much strength as I could, I threw his arm over my head, placed my other hand on his back, and slammed the man down to the ground.

His hand fell on the ground as he slipped into unconsciousness.

"Sorry about this. Nothing personal, but I need your tools," I said to him. It was true, too.

As a torch runner, this guy carried around a bag full of flammable liquids in large quantities, and matches

I grabbed all of his supplies and warped inside another small building—the same shop I had come crashing through the last time I was at the palace. The roof was just starting to be repaired. I felt bad for the shop owner as I poured some of the liquid out on the fine clothing and struck the match.

I'm not sure what was inside the torch runner's container, but it was strong. Very strong. The smell burned the inside of my nose. I dropped the match, and everything around me caught ablaze faster than I could have ever imagined.

I warped back out of the store and reappeared on top of a nearby building. From where I stood, looking down, I could see the flames dancing in the night, somehow resistant to the rain as it fell.

I looked down in the torch runner's bag. He had around six more containers of the liquid, which meant I would have to do the same thing to at least six more buildings near the palace.

In what seemed like no time, my bag was empty. I stood on a high building and watched as the neighborhood burned. It pained me some to see my home of Thera ablaze, but the contract must be fulfilled. For myself, for my family, and for Ember, wherever he was.

I made sure all the buildings were empty before I set them on fire, and realized that each bottle contained enough for two buildings to burn strongly. I don't know what this stuff was, but it was dangerous in the wrong hands. A torch runner could take out half a kingdom if they felt like it.

The rain continued to fall, but the various fires continued to burn bright. It still proved to be resistant to rain water, or perhaps I had used too much of the liquid to set the fires; either way, I had to wait for the rest of the plan to unfold. It didn't take long for the palace gates to open, and an army of guards flowed out in various directions.

Some were on foot, some were being carried in carriages, while others rode on the backs of caprongs. A total of eleven buildings were burning, and they were spread out enough that it would take the guards some time to contain them. Even foot patrol guards from around Thera were running to the scene.

It had worked. The guards, or at least most of them, had left the palace to control the fires before they started to spread. I wished I could take credit for this, but it was Rema's plan. A plan she had come up with ease. I wondered if she had had this plan already in her head for some other reason.

I looked the palace over and tried to remember, from where I was, the general direction of the Emperor's sleeping quarters. According to Rema, with all of the guards putting out fires, the remaining guards would push the Emperor and his wife to their rooms and guard them well.

I let my eyes rest on a third floor area with seating for palace guests. I allowed my foot to step off the ledge and warped. For a split second, there was silence, and no rain.

"What?" I said to myself as I appeared in the outside seating area. I looked around in the rain, dagger in hand. I could feel myself breathing heavily as I tried to figure out what had just happened and what I had heard.

For a moment, for that fraction of a second when I'd warped, I'd thought I'd heard a voice before I'd reappeared. That couldn't be possible, though, could it? I didn't have time to worry about it now. I pocketed my dagger and ran to the wall of the palace. I looked up and, about three more floors up, I could see a window. This was the same side that I had jumped from, and looking at this wall, it was the same way that Craydon Addersfield and his partner had climbed up.

The wall was slick from rain and my hands were just as wet. I climbed, though. One hand after the other, one foot at a time. I slowly climbed up. One story, and then I passed the second story. The seating area was already three floors up, and from there I climbed up three more levels. I was almost six floors up on a building that had, easily, ten floors. All I needed to do was be able to see inside the window, and I could warp inside.

I was so close that I could feel my heart skip a beat. I raised my hand for the final time to grab a part of the wall that stuck out some. I was almost there—and then my hand slipped, causing me to fall, and my feet began to kick as I tried to find a secure place to put them.

My feet continued to kick and flail as I hung on the side of the wall with one hand. I was capable of many things, but feats of strength were not one of them. I tried to pull myself up, but nothing happened. My arm began to burn as I could feel my little bit of grip slowly start to give away under the strain.

I looked down, and had no other choice. I warped back to the ground on the rooftop seating area. I stepped back and looked at the wall once more. I could have just warped to a spot on the wall, but that would require a precisely-timed grab on my part. I knew my limits, and that wasn't going to be something I could do.

With time running out, I began to ascend the wall again. This time up, it seemed easier than before. I didn't slip, and the rain on the wall that got on my hands didn't seem to hinder me at all. When I came to the window for the floor I was looking for, I immediately recognized it as the same hall I had fought the Battle Born female on.

I peered inside, making sure I wasn't going to have any surprises. As I had hoped, it was empty. I warped inside, reappearing a mere foot or two away from the window. My cloak was soaked, and clung to me as I tried to get some of the excess water off. I dropped my hood and checked my knives.

If memory served me correctly, the Emperor's hall wasn't too far. A few turns and I would be there. I moved quickly down the lit corridor, making almost no sound. As I came to the first corner, I saw two guards walk by. I clung to the wall beside me, staying as close to the shadows as possible. They didn't seemed to have seen me, and they were moving in the opposite direction. Maybe they were the guards for the Emperor's room and were going on a patrol.

My hopes faded away as I came to the last turn in my trip. I stepped down the hall and recognized the door immediately. There it was—looming, tall and black. Behind those doors waited my prey, and my job would be fulfilled once it was over.

The only problem was the ten guards standing in my way. Not only were there ten guards, but they all seemed to be from different kingdoms. Most were brandishing different weapons, and they were all looking directly at me.

23

I could feel the lump in my throat move as I swallowed. I took a step back for a second, foolishly hoping they hadn't seen me, but as I took that step, they all took a small step forward. So much for that idea.

The guards didn't just stand in front of the door; they had a formation to them. Each guard was spread out, and placed one behind the other as they stretched down the corridor leading to the large door I needed to get inside. They were prepared for me. They were prepared to fight a Warper.

Warpers were feared by most, and respected by some. Needless to say, you didn't go looking for a fight with a Warper. However, some knew the secret to fighting us. Some knew that, one on one, a Warper almost always won. It was just too hard to lock us down, but with multiple opponents, in close quarters, the fight tilted out of our favor.

One against ten was almost impossible. Because of how they were spread out, no matter where I warped to, I would be reappearing in front of another, and within arm's reach. I took a deep breath and drew my dagger. Each guard looked as if they had only one goal in life, and that was to end mine.

I had to give the Empress credit for being original. Instead of just having guards from the palace protect the door, she had created her own personal squad. A crew that seemed comprised of guards and fighters from different regions of The Prime Sovereignty.

I knew my life could end right here in this corridor.

While the rest of my friends, Vida, Jolin, and the Thornes, were sitting comfortably in the safe house, waiting for my return and the news of the Emperor and Empress's deaths, I could die tonight. I'd never see my mother again, or my siblings.

Before I could think about it anymore, one guard, holding metal rod-like weapons, jumped at me. The fact that he had covered such a large distance with a single leap was amazing. As he came crashing down, so did his metal rods.

I warped to the side and he missed me by inches. It looked impressive, but I had warped out of reflex, not skill. As I reappeared, the man swung a metal rod at my shin, and pain spread through my leg. It was as if I wasn't even wearing my greaves for protection. I stumbled some as the man followed up with two more blows. I dodged them both, and turned my body to punch the man, but before I could, I heard a loud pop and felt something wrap around my wrist.

It was a whip. A guard had grabbed my punch out of the air and stopped it.

As I let my eyes follow the whip around my wrist and back to its owner, three things happened all in succession. The man with the metal rods hit me in the stomach at the exact same time that I felt an arrow puncture my shoulder. Before I could try to remove the arrow from my shoulder, the man with the whip jerked me to him, jumped in the air, raised his fist, and delivered it to the side of my face.

I could feel my body spin in the air as I landed on the ground and rolled. My hands were free now, and the arrow had broken off as I found the ground. My body hurt on many levels, and pain was everywhere at once. This was the second time in only a short period of time that I had found myself losing a fight in this corridor.

The pain in my stomach made it hard to breathe, my

head was hurting, and I couldn't even remove the arrow from my shoulder because the end had broken off.

I pushed myself up slowly to one knee as I watched my attackers. All this, and I had only faced three of the ten. A few were even laughing to each other in the back. A guard from Pradeep pulled out another arrow and drew it in his bow, while the guard with the metal rod weapons spat on the ground.

"This is the Warper causing so much trouble for the Empress?" He spat on the ground once more.

Fine. I'd known it would happen someday, and I had held it off for as long as I could, but now it was me or them. Curse be damned. The time for fists had passed.

I drew my dagger in one hand. I stood tall, trying to push the pain away, as the man twirled his rods with a smirk.

"Come on, boy," he said to me. The guard behind him was wrapping his whip up, coiling it like a snake ready to strike.

For the first time in my life, I was ready to kill. To take a life, all of their lives, if it meant saving my own. I didn't have Ember to protect me, and maybe I never would again. This was my fight, and mine alone.

Dagger in hand, I warped.

The guard from Pradeep was the first target to feel my blade. Just like a guard with a spear, he would be vulnerable up close. I reappeared behind him. I had to move fast, because the man with the whip, along with over half a dozen other guards, were behind me. I grabbed the Pradeep guard's head as I appeared and plunged my knife into his neck.

That was it. I could feel the man's body shake and go limp. He was dying, and the curse had started as his warm blood flowed over my hands. My blade went in so deep that my hand was against his neck, no blade in sight. As Ember had always instructed, I moved the blade slightly inside his neck and then pulled it back out. Blood poured down his body.

I warped again to where I had once stood before his body even hit the floor.

The guard with the whip was fast. As I reappeared, I heard the pop, and felt the snake-like whip wrap around my body. Before he could pull me down, I reached behind my back for my belt, found a throwing knife, and sent it flying to the man's face. It found its mark, right between his eyes, and it was buried handle-deep. His grip on the whip loosened as he fell.

I tried to get the whip off of myself, but before I could, I felt a pain in my back that sent me in the direction of the normal palace guards. They swung with their swords. I warped out of their way, only to be struck again by the man with the metal rods. He was becoming a nuisance. I threw a throwing knife at him, but he knocked it away as he held his rods up across his face, making a shield for himself.

I warped again as he advanced; this time I appeared behind one of the palace guards, and drove my dagger into his back three times, leaving it in his back the third time and using his body as a shield of my own, as his fellow guard swung at me with his sword.

His sword found its mark as I ducked down low, and the guard I was using for a shield had his head removed by the swing of the other guard. Blood and chunks fell from where the man's head had once been and poured over me. It was in my mouth and my eyes, but I had to keep moving.

The second guard, still in shock from decapitating his fellow, had allowed his sword to drop some as he looked at the head on the floor. I warped, reappearing beside him and spinning as I extended my dagger on the outer arc, slashing his neck open in the process. As I spun, more blood that wasn't mine fell on me, and I could see large guards from Kameace backing up to the door they were sent to protect.

Six. Six guards were left. I picked up the fallen guard's sword. Sword in hand, I advanced on the man with metal rods. I wasn't familiar with a sword as much as I was a dagger, but he didn't know that. We clashed in the middle of the corridor, his metal rods colliding with my sword, sparks flying.

I swung my sword and he parried it with his first metal rod, spun around and hit me in the back again with the second. I lost my footing and slashed at the man again, but he ducked under my sword, used one rod to hit me in the stomach, and as I fell over in pain, he brought another rod up from the ground, and it found its mark under my chin.

I heard the sword in my hand fall to the ground as I was sent flying and landed on my back. He ran to me, rods in hand, as I reached for my last throwing knife. I sent it his way, but from this position I knew it was a horrible attack, one that he blocked with ease with the wave of his rod. As he blocked it, I warped from where I was on the ground, removed my other throwing knife from the whip guard's head, and warped again. I appeared behind the man with metal rods, and plunged my throwing knife into his skull. Once in his skull, I broke the handle off, leaving nothing but the blade inside.

The man fell, and so did his metal rods. As they clanged on the ground and rolled away, I allowed myself a moment to rest against the wall. I was hurt, had a bleeding shoulder, and was covered in blood that wasn't mine, but I was alive. I looked at the handle in my hand. I had really liked my throwing knives, and now I was one short. I would have to get a new set if I made it out of this.

I stood up and turned to the Kameace guards.

They said nothing, but held their clubs up to their sides. I collected my other weapons and removed some of the blood from my face.

"Do you really want to die here tonight? Alone in a corridor far from your homes? From your families?"

The guards looked at each other.

"Step aside," I said. "Return to your Kingdom, and you won't have to die tonight."

Nothing happened as they tried to figure out what to. I exhaled, and threw a throwing knife at them, purposefully missing and finding my mark at the door behind them. They lowered their clubs and began to move. "Leave your weapons," I said calmly, and they did. They placed them on the floor at their feet and slowly walked away, watching me, as if they thought I still would attack.

I slowly walked to the door. I was actually limping more than walking, but this was it. I ignored the pain in my stomach, my back, and tried not to think about the arrow inside my shoulder. I came to the door and tried the knob.

It was locked. I dropped to one knee, and, as before, peered through the keyhole and warped inside.

24

I ran full speed down the entrance hall and found the two separate rooms again. For some reason, I expected both the Empress and Emperor to be standing behind the door, waiting for me. That would have been too easy, though.

I checked the Empress' room first, since she seemed to be the one running everything. It was empty, but in disarray. Her bed looked as if somebody had been recently sleeping in it, and she had clothes all over the place.

"No, no, no," I said as I ran to the second room.

As I came in, someone inside jumped.

It was the Emperor, or whoever had been changed into the Emperor.

"So, finally come to kill me, have you?" he said as he slowly turned and looked at me. It was different. I had seen Vida change before, so I knew the level of skill Changelings possessed, but this man looked like the Emperor. He looked like the Emperor before him, and he looked like the first Anavor Nal. Same short blond hair. The same brown eyes. Except, now, he didn't have the same dominating posture. I would have never noticed it had I not known the truth, but all accounts said that before his first death, the Emperor was ruthless, and killed with no regard to life.

He was truly a beast, but when he had returned, he had seemed more controlled, and his wife, the Empress, had helped him. Helped him control, with intelligence. She was the true ruler all along. These men were just puppets. I had begun to guess that she was the creator of The Battle Born, too. I didn't know how, but she had to have been behind those things as well.

"She's gone, you know," the man said as he sat down on his bed. "When she heard the noise outside, she left through a secret passage in her room. You just missed her, actually." He seemed so calm. He spoke to me, a person covered in blood, dagger drawn, as if we were old friends.

He rubbed his hand over the bed slightly. "You know, she never even allowed me to sleep in this room. Apparently she and the first Emperor didn't share a bed, yet she never allowed the room to be used after."

"Where is she going?" I asked him.

"I'm not sure," he said with a shrug.

I didn't want to kill him. I know it was the contract, but he wasn't the person doing these things. The abductions, the killing, the secrets about people beyond the water. It was all the Empress.

"Where is the passageway?" I asked him as I moved to turn.

"I'm not sure about that either, but it leads to the main hall."

Good, I thought to myself. I knew where that was and how to get there. I even had an idea about a shortcut. I turned away from him and began to exit the room.

"Wait," he said from the bed as he stretched his hand up. It wasn't a command—more so a plea. "Kill me. Please."

I looked at him. His eyes were glossy and red now as a tear rolled down his face.

"I was a normal man once. A palace worker, actually. I had a wife, and five children. All girls." He said this last part with a smile as he wiped his face. "When the Emperor before me died, it was around the time that I was begging other palace workers for food, yolars, and any type of help.

The Empress knew, and offered me a way to support my family."

The more he wiped his face, the more the tears ran down. His voice was broken now and his face was distorted as he tried to talk through the pain. He gasped for his breath.

"She said all I had to do was agree to play the part, and my family would be well taken care of and given a home in Pradeep. So I agreed. I told my wife everything and made her swear not to tell.

"I wasn't allowed to see them, so I wrote them letters. Almost every day. Then, one day, I began to notice that the letters I received from her didn't sound right. The words on the paper were words my wife would never use. People here believed me to be the true Emperor. A reborn immortal. They feared me, and did what I asked with no questions. So, in secret, I sent people to search for my family. It was then that I found out they never made it to Pradeep."

I could feel my breath hitch as I turned away from him slightly.

"She had them killed. All of them. Almost as soon as I was changed." The Emperor rocked a little as he began to sob. "When I confronted her, she didn't deny it. She told me the rest of my family would meet the same fate if I didn't play the role. She said she would kill anybody who shared a hint of my blood." He shook his head. "I was a coward. So please—end this and allow me to see my family again with The Keeper."

I walked to him as he continued to sob. I had to blink a few times to clear my vision, and I could feel the air in the room cooling the tears on my cheek. I placed a hand on his shoulder as I stood in front of him. It was stained with dried blood. To my surprise, he grabbed my hand and squeezed it. "Thank you," he said between sobs and sniffs.

In a firm thrust, I allowed my dagger to find his heart. His grip on my hand went limp as his body relaxed. It was fast, and painless. I allowed his body to lay on the bed. He looked as if he were simply sleeping. The Emperor was dead, and after tonight there wouldn't be another to take his place.

I ran from the room at full speed, and returned to the Empress' room. Looking from her window I could see, with surprise, that many of the flames continued to burn around the palace. This meant I still had some time. I looked down, and from here could see the entrance to the palace. The same entrance that we had used to enter for the ball in the main hall.

I locked my eyes on the ground down there. It seemed so far, and was barely visible through the rain, but the fires I had created gave the lower parts of the palace an eerie glow. Enough glow for me to see where I was going. I warped, traveling from the room of the Empress to the palace grounds in an instant.

I heard it again. A voice, before I reappeared. This time I was a little more positive than I had been the last time, but I still couldn't make out what it said, and it was over too fast.

As the rain fell, I could smell the smoke from the fires in the air, and in the distance I could hear people screaming and guards marching. As I spun around I could see why the fires were still going. They weren't the fires I had caused, but they were different. The fires had spread.

In Rema's plan, she had believed that the fires would last long enough for me to complete the job, but the rain would eventually put them out. She was wrong. The rain did nothing, and even with the guards trying, the fires raged on. Spreading to surrounding homes and shops. Spreading to people. Thera was burning.

"What have you done?" I heard a woman scream behind me. Turning, I saw her.

Red hair stuck to her head from rain, and her white sleeping gown was covered in dirt and clung to her. She was barefoot and breathed as if she had been running nonstop.

Empress Selen Nal had finally made it out of the palace.

She had a look of surprise and anger on her face as she snarled at me, but took a step away from me. "Guards!" she screamed, but nothing happened. The fires had made sure they were busy. She continued to move away from me.

I warped and appeared behind her. She looked around wildly as she saw me vanish. She kept backing up, making her way back to the palace, and then she bumped into me. She let out a scream as she turned to me.

"I know everything," I said as I dropped my hood. I didn't care if rain and blood got in my eyes. I wanted her to see me.

It was odd. I once had dreaded killing, but now, it seemed natural. I held this dagger in my hand and I knew she was going to die. These final moments would be the Empress' last breaths.

"The Emperor, or whoever he really was, is already dead, Thera burns, and your rule has come to an end. I even know about the boats, and the people beyond the waters."

Her eyes grew wide and she stammered as she tried to speak. "She—"

Her words were cut off as I stabbed her twice. Once in the stomach, and once in the neck. Ember had always said to never let your victim speak. They would do anything to save their lives.

He had taught me so much, and now he wasn't here to see this.

The Empress fell to the ground, clasping at her neck.

"Rema," she said as she gasped.

My neck twitched as my head jerked to her. "What?" I said as I dropped down and held her head up. "Rema what?" I yelled at her.

"She controls, she controls." Her eyes stared up at me, blank. Lifeless. The hand she held to her own bleeding throat fell limp and touched the ground as rain continued to fall on her face.

I left her on the ground. What was she trying to say? Rema controlled what?

I pulled my hood up. It looked like Rema Thorne, and perhaps even her brother, had some things to answer for. Something was going on, and I needed to find out.

"Arrest him," a voice called out.

I knew that voice before I even raised my head to face it. It was Rema.

I pulled my hood down as I slowly looked up. Standing before me, in full battle armor that seemed to shine from the rain and the glow from the fire, was Rema Throne. She rode a caprong, and had several guards with her. For the first time, she looked like royalty.

She had a grin on her face, and so did the guard to her side. It was Quarts, her servant from the safe house. He had on armor as well. Clearly, he had never been a servant at all.

Behind them, tied and gagged, were Vida and Jolin, both thrown over the back of caprongs and riding with guards. Jolin seemed to be unconscious, while Vida moved as much as she could and tried to get away. It was useless, though. She, like Jolin, wasn't going anywhere.

"This Warper and his friends have plotted against The Prime Sovereignty, killed the Empress, and set Thera ablaze," Rema said as she pointed.

I glanced at Vida again, who had eyes wide open towards me. I could hear her voice in my head, screaming for me to get away.

"We have gotten word from inside the palace that The Emperor is dead too," Rema shouted as more guards on caprongs appeared from the darkness. "As the only high noble in Thera, I have assumed command until the Emperor is reborn." She knew he wouldn't be reborn, though. She knew the Empress was a changeling, just like I did. Just like we all did.

I looked around as everything began to fall into place. This—this had been her plan all along. As the rain fell, my shoulder began to hurt again. All the excitement and adrenaline from fighting had worn off, and pain was flooding my body.

In my head I could hear Remy arguing with his sister. *They trust us. They have always trusted us, and you want to betray them.* At the time I had thought he was upset at the betrayal of the Emperor and the Empress, because his sister had wanted them killed. Now, slamming into me, was the wave of realization: he had been talking about us. Jolin, me, Vida, and Ember. *Ember*, I thought to myself.

She had sent him away. Sent him to some place he hadn't returned from. It was all the plan from the start. She had fooled us all, and now here she was ready to take control, and her first action would be to bring us to justice. No wonder Jolin was gagged and knocked out. She couldn't allow him to speak.

I had to get out of here.

I looked at Rema once more. She smiled at me. That same smile that I had always felt was rehearsed. Why was she smiling? She knew I could warp away. She wouldn't be able to stop me.

I took a deep breath as fear—uncontrolled, unmatched fear—rolled over my body. I tried to warp, and I couldn't. I felt emptiness inside again. I looked up to Rema once more and saw it. Behind her, behind the guards that held my friends captive, was a silhouette, barely visible through the rain.

I couldn't make it out, but what I could make out were two glowing purple eyes. Rema had brought a Battle Born with her.

I only saw one way out of this. It wasn't the choice I wanted to make, but I had to be smart. I shot a glare at Rema, and then I ran.

PART III

25

Fear is an amazing source of energy. I was tired, bruised, bloody, and in pain, but fear, fear and anger like I had never felt before, kept me standing and moving. It was possible that Rema expected me to fight. To stand my ground and try to save my friends. This was the first time she had been wrong in her schemes.

I couldn't defeat them all, even if I had my powers, but with a Battle Born in their midst, I stood no chance. I did the only thing I could do. I ran. Rema and her men were blocking my way to Thera, so I turned and ran into the palace. It wasn't ideal, but I didn't have many options at that point.

I was lucky that none of the guards with her had spears, or my sprint to the palace would have been short-lived. I felt wind and water hitting my face as I ran, trying not to slip on wet stones beneath my feet. Rema had screamed something; I was moving too fast to hear what it was, but I could guess.

I glanced over my shoulder as I ran through the palace courtyard and saw several of the guards getting off their caprongs. The Battle Born was too far away to see. It was that thing I had to outrun. Once I got away from the radius of its powers, I could warp away and figure out what to do.

I made my way inside and headed to the main hall of the palace. Aside from a few workers, who screamed and got out of my way as I ran, the palace was empty. No guards yet, thankfully.

As I approached the end of the hall, I could hear the

door at the other end burst open.

"Find him!" a voice screamed. I didn't stick around to see if it were accompanied by the Battle Born, or if they were even following me. I just continued to run, this time down the corridor Vida and I had entered when we were here for the ball.

I found a window quickly. The palace corridors were full of them. I looked out and found fires still cutting through the darkness. I reached inside myself and found that power again, but it was faint.

The surrounding corridor around me was no more as I warped away, finding my destination on a building directly beside a few others that were burning brightly. I had only burned one building in this area, but it had traveled to five others. I hated to see Thera burn, but at least it was in this area, near the palace. Owners of these houses and shops would be able to rebuild. I just hoped nobody lost her lives because of the part I had played.

I could feel the heat rising up from the flames, and the air was almost impossible to breathe. I looked at my shoulder for a moment. It was throbbing now. I needed to get this looked at.

I turned and warped from the building before it fell victim to the flames around it. Again and again I warped, covering almost half of the city in what seemed like seconds. I knew where I was heading, and I was almost there.

Reappearing on a building across the street, I looked down at the little house. My home. There were no guards around, and this portion of Thera seemed untouched by the events at the Palace. Tomorrow, when the rest of Thera awoke, they would see how the world had changed.

I warped to the street below and peered inside of a

window. It was mostly covered by a curtain, but through a small opening I could see that my mother was up. This surprised me. What was she doing up at this time of night? She was sitting alone at the table, drinking from a cup by a low-burning lantern. She and the twins were safe for now. Rema didn't know about them or where they lived. She barely knew about me—because Ember was the Warper they had wanted, not me.

My mother squealed and jumped as I reappeared in the room beside her. Her mouth dropped open, and she covered it with her hands as I lowered my hood.

"Hey mom," I said, wincing as I removed my cloak.

"Lox," she said. She quickly got from her seat and helped me take off my cloak.

She threw it to the floor and sat me down at the table. She rubbed her hands on my face and looked at me.

"What happened? Where's Ember?" she asked as she looked to the rest of the room. She was expecting him to appear.

"I don't know," I said as I removed my bloody shirt. "He may be dead."

Her face turned up and her eyes grew red. Then she saw my shoulder.

"Oh, no," she said as she looked at my arm. "How did—"

"It's a long story, mom," I said, cutting her off. "Where are Luka and Kula?" "They're sleeping," she said as she looked at my shoulder from front to back. "No exit wound."

She moved to the kitchen for a second and returned with some water, rags, and medicine.

"Lox, what happened to you?" she asked, placing a knife over the fire of the uncovered lantern.

"What are you doing?" I asked, but I already knew. I

suddenly longed for Jolin and his medical kit. My mom knew what she was doing; raising me and the two twins had given her practice with wounds, but it wasn't going to be pleasant.

"Sterilizing," she said as she removed the knife from the flame. "We have to get that arrowhead out." She handed me one of the many cloths she had returned with. "Bite down on this, and you'd better not wake the twins."

I did as I was told and placed the cloth in my mouth and bit down as hard as I could. The knife felt hotter than the sun as it entered my wound. My mouth watered as I bit down. I clenched my fist so tightly that, when it was finally over, my hand was sore.

After a few moments of digging, the arrow, reflecting light from the fire, lay on the table. The pain from the hole it had left behind was still there, but at least it was out.

My mother took a bowl and mixed water and something else inside to clean the wound. "There's so much blood," she said as she looked me over.

"If it makes you feel better, mom, it's not all mine," I said as I tried to smile.

"It doesn't," she replied as she continued to clean the wound. Whatever was mixed with the water burned, but was slowly taking the pain away from the hole in my shoulder.

"Now tell me what happened."

"I don't think—"

She stopped cleaning and looked at me sternly. I was starting to think this was an ability all mothers had. The look that made you afraid and, at the same time, comforted you, to let you know that everything, for the moment, would be okay.

For now, I wasn't a Warper, or an assassin. I was

simply her son. Her hurt son, and she wanted answers. So I told her everything. In the hour that followed she continued to dress my wound. Cleaning it, covering it with some sticky stuff to help speed up the healing. In return I told her everything.

I told her about Jolin, Vida, and the Thornes. I told her about the murders, about the Emperor, and finally I told her how I had killed them. This last part was what made her stop. She knew what I was. Ember had told her years ago. She knew what I was destined to do, and she had never liked it. Now, she was finally seeing what my world was like when I left her and the twins behind.

She gave me an old shirt she had found for me to wear.

"Do you still have the yolars I left you?"

She nodded as she began to clean up the table.

"Good. Take it and the twins and get out of Thera. Walden should be safe for you."

"Okay," she replied as she finished cleaning up. I had expected some level of resistance from her, considering that Thera has been the only home she has ever known.

"How long will it take you to get ready?" she asked me.

"Get ready?" I repeated.

"We're going to Walden, right?" she said as she looked at me. I could see it in her eyes. They darted around the room, and then focused on me. They were wide and glossy. "Lox," she said as her voice cracked.

I stood from the table and walked to her. "Mom, I can't leave."

"You can," she said. "You're my son, and—and you have to do what I say."

"I can't. I have to put an end to this."

"But why you? You could leave this life. We can be a family again and start over."

I shook my head. If only it was that easy. I was sure Rema would continue to look for me, and if my family was with me, I would be putting them in danger, too. I had started this and I was going to have to try to finish it.

"I was born to do this. Literally. I can't just stop now. It's who I am, mom. I can't turn back now. Not when Jolin and Vida still need me."

We were silent for a few moments. I couldn't tell what she was thinking.

I looked at her. "You guys need to get out of Thera. I'll find you when this is all over. If you don't hear from me within in six days—"

I couldn't bring myself to say it, but she knew. She just shook her head some and kissed me on the cheek.

"I love you, mom," I said slowly, trying not to let my voice give me away.

"I love you too, son. Whatever happens, know that I'm proud of you, and even with this curse, I know you will do great things."

The next morning, I sat down once more at the table and looked around the now-empty house. It seemed so big now that I was alone. I had found some more of the old clothes my mom had stashed away. The trousers I wore were smaller than usual, but for the most part they still fit me well. Before she left, she made sure I had food to eat.

I had only begun to eat some of the soup she'd left for me when I heard a knock at the door.

I took in two more spoons-full and then grabbed my dagger and warped to the door. I crouched low and peeked out the window. No guards were there. The knock came again. Seeing as I couldn't see them from the window, it must have been just one person. I hid my dagger and opened the door slowly.

Instantly I could feel my face getting hot as anger pushed rational thought away from me. Standing there, on the doorstep, was Remy Thorne. He was also holding Sprits in his arms.

"Thank the Keeper. I was starting to think I had the wrong house," he said. "Can I come in?"

I grabbed Sprits from him and placed him inside. Remy kept looking around on the outside. I stuck my head out and peered around the street. Everything seemed normal. People were walking by, a few carriage were moving off in the distance, and, lightly, the snow was falling. I grabbed Remy by his throat and pulled him in the house, shutting the door so hard behind him that the house felt like it was shaking.

"What are you doing here?" I asked him as I placed the tip of my dagger to his throat.

He looked down at the dagger and then back to me as he put his hands up. "Let me explain," he said slowly.

"Explain? You think you can explain why your sister betrayed us?" I screamed the words at him.

"I never wanted any of this to happen. I was against it from the start," he stammered.

"You let it happen. You could have warned us. Warned Ember. I should cut your head off and deliver it to her," I said, removing the tip of the dagger and replacing it with its edge. "I could do it. Remy Thorne, high noble, killed in the slums of Thera. Fitting end." These last words were hissed more than spoken.

"My sister and I have never seen eye to eye. You know that. If you think back to when this all started, in Pradeep—I told her she didn't have to do this." He was right. I did remember him saying that to his sister, but I had thought he was talking about everything that was about to come.

"Lox, you have to believe me. I want to stop her as much as you."

"Then tell me the truth. Tell me what's really going on," I said as I stepped back from him, dagger still raised. "Believe me when I tell you—if you try anything, I will kill you, Remy."

26

"I suggest you start by telling me how you even knew where to find me," I said as Remy moved to sit down. He was followed by Sprits, who leaned on his leg. They seemed to be getting along better than ever. As everything had been going on, I had forgotten about Sprits. At least he was being taken care of.

"I've known where you lived from the moment Ember brought you to us," Remy replied. "When you showed up with him, you were an unexpected addition to our ranks, and I wanted to know as much about you as I could. Just to be safe."

I glanced at the door, and then to some of the windows in the room. He seemed to read my mind and knew what I was thinking.

"I didn't tell anybody where you were from. You don't have to worry about that," he said as he leaned forward and put his elbows on his knees. "A man should feel safe in his home. I wouldn't take that away from you, Lox."

"If only your sister thought like you did," I said as I sat down at the table. "So what's going on out there?" I asked him. "Was any of it true? Or was your sister just stringing us along the entire time?"

He turned from me slightly. He looked odd as he searched for the words to say. His hands kept moving, as if he was used to holding something that wasn't there now. A book, I was sure. This was one of the rare times I had seen Remy without a book in hand.

"Yes," he said suddenly. "Some of it was true. There

was a person who arrived in our lands from beyond the waters. He had others with him, and traveled in something called a boat." He paused as he tried to calm his hands. Remy began to clasp them together to keep them from moving.

"Then there were parts that weren't true, and parts that were left out."

"Well, explain," I said as I locked my eyes on him.

"First, the few men that arrived in our lands in a boat. They claimed they had traveled across the waters in a larger boat that they called a ship.

"When they arrived, the Emperor didn't discover them, but some of our workers did. We owned the land they landed on and, before we notified the Emperor, Rema spent days talking to them and learning from them. Then she killed the few she had talked to, and turned the others over to the Emperor."

"So why all of this? Why go kill the Emperor?"

"Rema has always had a lust for power." He laughed a little. "When she found out there were other lands beyond ours, she urged the Emperor and Empress to use these people and to spread our control. Naturally, they declined her, and it was then that her plan was put in motion. To overthrow the Emperor, and to secretly venture out into this new world."

I opened my mouth, but he raised his hands.

"There is more." He looked almost afraid now as his eyes got wide, and his leg began to shake a little. "These people, from beyond the water, said they didn't find us by accident. They told us that their god had sent them. A god other than the Keeper."

"That's it?" I said as I laughed. Remy looked at me with a flat expression, mouth open slightly. "I don't believe in all that. So let's not fear them just because these people have decided to believe in unseen forces."

He nodded, but still looked at me in surprise. Clearly he had expected me to be afraid, as he was, at the idea of a god outside the Keeper.

"What does she intend to do to Vida and Jolin?" I asked him.

He stood up and waved his hands as he moved around. "I don't know. She is spreading the lie that all of you were involved in an elaborate plot. A plot where Jolin was the mastermind." That was unexpected.

"How is she going to make people believe that? What reason would Jolin have to try to have the Emperor killed?" Remy exhaled and looked away from me. "Remy," I said, following him when he walked away.

"Jolin," he said, "is a noble. Well, he was a noble, anyway."

I shook my head as I laughed slightly. "Jolin is a lot of things. Good at patching you up if you're cut. Unusually polite. But he isn't a noble."

"You're right and wrong. Jolin's family was originally of high noble status. Higher than that of mine, I'm afraid." I could tell from his face that Remy was serious. There wasn't a flicker of laughter or a hint of a smile. "Jolin's family was stripped of their status, wealth, and possessions, before he was even born, by the Emperor's father. Jolin's family, disgraced as they were, fled from Thera to start a new life in Galcon. It wasn't until Jolin realized that he was a Tongue that he began collecting secrets, hoping to find a way to restore his family's name. My sister promised him that his family's name would be restored when this was all done."

I hadn't expected this. Jolin, a noble? If this was true, it made him an easy person to place the blame on, and to take the fall for Rema's plan. Jolin would never be allowed to speak out against the accusations.

I could feel myself begin to panic. "What about Vida?" I asked.

"She is likely to face the same outcome as Jolin," Remy replied. I looked at him silently. "Execution," he said slowly.

"Execution?" I repeated. "How soon?"

"Tomorrow morning. In front of the council, and the upper classes of Thera. They are being held at the council's building under heavy guard, so when the time comes, there won't be a long wait. Rema's idea."

Tomorrow. That was soon, but it did give me some time to try to get them out. I had no idea how to rescue them. This wasn't what Warpers did, and we certainly weren't known for our ability to halt murders.

I put my belt on and placed my dagger and throwing knives on the table.

"If you really want to help, I need you to talk to as many people as you can and tell them what is really going on."

Remy didn't seem too keen on this idea. "Rema has many supporters, and those that don't support her still accept bribes from her," he replied.

"Many isn't the same as all," I said to him as I began to sharpen my dagger.

"Tell as many people as you can, and try to halt the execution. I don't need you to really stop it, because I'm going to get them out."

"How?" he asked.

It was a good question. One which I had no answer to. There wasn't enough time to research the council building thoroughly enough to make the plan work, but I needed to figure out something.

"I'll figure it out," I told him as I pointed to the door.

"You just head there now and convince as many people that you can that Rema was behind it all. Give them proof if you have it."

He looked at me blankly one last time, as if he was waging an internal battle in his head. Then he slowly nodded as he picked up Sprits and went for the door.

"Remy," I said as he opened the door. He was almost out, and had to lean around the door to see me. "Your sister."

He shook his head in agreement. "She's done horrible things. Do what you must. I hold no grudges." He left my home, and gently shut the door behind him.

I continued to sharpen my blades. With what was coming, and the sheer amount of people who were going to die, the last thing I wanted during this insane rescue attempt was a dull blade. I was almost done when I heard a knock at the door again.

I jerked it open. "Forget something?" I said, in a mocking tone. But when the door opened, I found that it wasn't Remy at all. It was a child. I had seen this child before, but I couldn't remember where. He had on dirty clothes, and looked up at me and smiled.

"Hello, Lox," he said as he flashed those white teeth. Then it hit me—he was the child on the street that I gave the yolar to as the fight broke out.

I looked at him with a grimace on my face. "How do you know my name?" I asked him. "Better yet, how do you know where I live?"

I slowly put my hand behind my back to reach for my dagger and found nothing. I cursed to myself. They were still on the table. Sharp and ready to go.

"I know many things," the boy said.

His voice didn't match his body. He sounded older than he appeared. "Maybe this body wasn't the best choice, but it was in this body that you were the nicest to me, so I thought it would make it easy."

He stepped back some and changed. This time, he was in the form of the extremely large man that had been asleep outside The Clarkton.

I could feel my brow rise. "You're a Changeling?" I said in shock.

He shook his head. "No. They are me," he replied, in the same voice, which now sounded too young for his body. "May I come in?"

"No. It's better if you tell me—"

My words were cut off as this boy, this changeling boy, now in the form of a man almost larger than my house, did something that should have been impossible. I knew it was coming, as I saw the air around him shift into a haze.

He warped.

Heart pounding, I turned and warped to my table, and grabbed a dagger. The boy was already inside the house, but in a different form. He stood before me with a smile on his face, those same unusually white teeth on display. He was a little shorter than me now, with smooth, light brown skin, and hair that was curly and unnaturally dark.

"What are you?" I asked as I kept my dagger on him. I tried not to, but I was beginning to panic. He was a Changeling, yet he was a Warper, too. Was that even possible? Just when I had thought this scene couldn't get any more complicated, I was proven wrong.

The boy, standing with a smile on his face, spoke as he waved his hand. "We don't have much time. I've seen what's to come, and you need to be ready for it. Even I can't change it." As he spoke, and moved his hand, my dagger warped from my hand and appeared in his.

"How?" I said as I felt sweat on my brow and my heart fell to my stomach. I looked at my empty hand. He was an inward Warper, *and* an outward Warper? Plus he was a—no. This couldn't be. I backed away slowly, trying to position myself near a window so that I could see a way out.

"You asked me what I was," the boy said casually as he sat down at the table and pulled another chair out for me. "The better question is *who* am I. An answer you will find hard to believe."

He looked at me as he propped his feet up on the table. I didn't move, and I surely wasn't about to join him at the table, but I asked anyway.

"Okay," I said slowly. "Who are you?"

"I have been called many things over the centuries, but long ago I was a simple farm boy who just wanted to play with his friends. In those times I was called Nasium Suro. My mother named me, don't insult it.

"Nobody has called me that for a long time, not since the beginning."

"So what should I call you?" I asked him. "Because you seem to know a lot about me."

He exhaled slightly and looked at me as he gestured for me to sit. I didn't.

"Most people these days refer to me as The Keeper."

27

"The Keeper?" I asked with a bemused grin on my face. I wanted to laugh, but, whether I believed him or not, he was powerful, whoever he was, and I had to choose my response carefully. "Not to insult you, but I'm having a hard time believing that—well, that you're a god."

He clasped his hands together as he sat at the table. He looked like a child waiting for more food at dinner.

"I expected as much from you. You are one of the few people who has never believed in me. Despite the amount of faith those close to you have. Your mother and Ember believe. Even you father believes in me."

"My father," I said.

He nodded slowly as he looked over the knives on the table. He rubbed his finger along one of the blades and winced for a second. Blood appeared on his skin.

It was there only for a second as the cut healed itself.

I could feel my face frowning as I watched him inspect his finger. "Gods bleed?" I asked him.

"I'm immortal, but not invincible. There's a difference. Now, please, sit down. A lot must happen in a short time, and it's easier if I show you some things instead of telling you."

He gestured for me to sit down once more as he displayed both fully-healed and scar-free hands. It was odd, hearing a child talk to me with such a demanding tone. He appeared to be younger, but had eyes of a person who had lived a hundred lifetimes. They were cold and deep eyes that seemed to look inside of me. These eyes were not those of a normal person.

He seemed to have a lot of knowledge about me, but even Remy had known where I lived, so any person with enough time could figure out private details about a person. Ember and I had done it time and time again. I couldn't explain the powers, though. How could he do some many things? It shouldn't have been possible, but then again, what did I know? Up until a few days ago, I hadn't even known Tongues and Changelings existed.

Against my better judgment, I sat down at the table anyway. As soon as I did, he warped. I found him standing behind me now, and for a second I reached for a knife on the table. Before I could get to the knife, I felt a hand on my shoulder, followed by a blinding light across my eyes and pain in my head.

Then there was nothing. No light, no pain, no sound. I could feel my eyes looking around, but I could see nothing. It was just darkness. Never-ending, unmoving darkness. I could faintly feel the hand on my shoulder still. It tightened, and then everything around me exploded to life. It was as if I was watching the world and the people living in it from outside a window.

I felt like I was moving with what I was seeing. As if I were there, but invisible. Everyone was moving at an increased speed. The lives I watched seemed to flash before me. For a second I saw a boy that looked just like the one who claimed he was The Keeper. He was wearing the same clothes, but his face was different. His eyes were different. They were youthful, full of happiness. He was running with three other children. Another boy and two girls.

I couldn't make their features out, for some reason. All four of them played in what seemed to be a field. The image changed quickly; the four children were now looking at what seemed to be a ripple in the air. Similar to the ones Warpers created, but on a larger scale. It was large, swirling, and black.

My nose suddenly burned. I could smell something. I was inside the hole in the air. It smelled of smoke, yet faintly of something sweet, too. I could hear a voice from one of the children—a girl, I thought—but I couldn't make out what she was saying. One of the four walked towards the hole and stretched his hand out. Something shot from the rippled air and surrounded his entire body, lifting him off the ground. The other children ran towards him to help. Their muffled voices grew louder as they faded away.

The image changed quickly again; now the four children stood atop a hill, looking at legions of people. No. It was less a hill, and more a mountain. More people than I had ever seen stretched across the land, all looking to them. The legion of people was chanting something, all in unison, but once again, I didn't know what. The air was cool on my skin up here. I could feel the energy from the four children as I stood with them. It radiated from them like ripples coming from a focal point in water.

Again I could see the face of the boy in my home. He looked worried as he glanced at his peers and then back to the land full of chanters. His peers all had smiles on their faces, but he seemed worried.

The scene faded away with another flash, this time revealing what seemed to be a war. I could smell the air again now. It was foul. A smell of death and blood. The odor was so strong that it seemed to be in my mouth.

It was snowing. Snow. I hadn't seen snow or rain in the previous images. Everything in front of me flashed again, and again I saw Nasium Suro. His face was different now. He looked tired. He stood alone on the shores with water behind him. Where were the others? He slowly turned and warped away, but I seemed to follow his warp as he reappeared. Now he was in a field. How had he warped so far without being able to see where he was going? From what I had seen seconds ago, there was no field to use as a warp point.

He looked around him and smiled for a moment, and then the snow came again. He looked up to the sky and frowned some, as if the snow was at fault. Nasium Suro placed his hand on the ground, and it became alive. What was once dark and lifeless became something more. It was grass. Lush, green, and vibrant, and it seemed to flow from his hand, growing on the ground around him. Not just grass, but trees, and flowers as well. He warped again, this time appearing in a different location. He closed his eyes for a moment, and something happened. He glowed for a moment. His entire body became a faint purple glow, and then he returned to normal.

Another flash. Now I could tell where I was. This was Thera, and I could see Nasium Suro, simply walking the streets in the rain. The rain—I could feel it on me. Cool, making my clothes cling to me. He continued to walk as he looked at the buildings and people walking by. He seemed happy, but his eyes were becoming more hollow. He stopped walking and seemed weak for a second; he had to lean against a wall for support.

Another flash, and then there was darkness again. When the darkness left, I saw some things all at once. They kept flickering and flashing so quickly that I couldn't make them out, and then I felt the hand move from my shoulder. As the hand lifted, so did the images, and I was back in my kitchen again.

I looked around as I tried to catch my breath. I stood

up so fast that I knocked my chair over and hit the table.

"What—what was that?" I asked him. Sweat, for some reason, ran down the side of my face.

He was sitting down again. "That was history. That, at the end, was the future. I'll admit the future is harder to see, because it's not fixed. It can be changed. But I have seen one outcome that is certain."

"What is it?" I asked him. It sounded more like a plea than a simple question.

"It's not important—" He was about to continue, but I interrupted.

"Not important?" I shouted.

He didn't seem to like this. He didn't react; he just looked at me, and I could feel those same waves of energy washing from him. It reminded me of the feeling I got when Jolin used his ability, but amplified.

"Sorry," I said.

He smiled. Then he allowed his face to become blank again, as if something else was bothering him. What bothered a god? Was I accepting that he was a god now?

"You will need to liberate your friends. Then we will speak again." He stood up from the table— a boy, only a little bigger than Luka. He seemed too frail to have such power.

"You're a god?" I said. It was more a question than a statement. "Are you? A god? Are you really, The Keeper?"

He clapped his hands together once, kept them together, and nodded to me. "The fact that you are even asking that means you are starting to believe. Now, before you try to free your friends and seek the vengeance I'm sure you will be after, warp across the room."

I looked at him, and then to the area he was pointing to. "You want me to warp?" I asked.

He remained passive. I looked across the room and reached inside myself to touch that power again. I felt it, and it was there, but this time, it wasn't alone. There was more. The power felt different. It felt stronger. It wasn't just in me—it *was* me. It pulsed over my body. I could feel it in my limbs, all the way to my fingertips.

I didn't move. I simply looked at him. "What did you do to me?"

"What is it the people of the kingdoms say now?" he asked. *"Blessed by the Keeper."* He shook his finger in the air. "I have augmented your abilities."

Nasium Suro. The Keeper. God. He shook his head and laughed a little under his breath.

"You are now the only person in the kingdoms able to both inwardly and outwardly warp. You can, like me, even warp another person along with you now."

I looked down at my hands as I turned them around. I didn't move, but I placed my eyes on a dagger near Nasium Suro. The same one that had cut him before. I reached inside myself once again, feeling that new energy. The air changed around the dagger only slightly before it vanished and appeared in my hand.

The dagger felt different than it had before. I turned it around in my hand. I could feel the smile grow on my face. "Why? Why me?" I asked as I continued to look at the dagger.

"I needed a hero," his voice replied faintly.

"Thank you," I said under my breath as I looked to the table, but he was gone now. Nasium Suro was the Keeper. God. Our god was real. He may have been a mere boy, but he was real, and he had just given me the ability to save my friends.

I warped my belongings to me. A simple gesture that I

took pride in. If only Ember could see me now. I didn't know if he was alive or not, but at least I knew there was a god who could possibly watch over him.

I adjusted my armor and checked my blades. I looked outside and watched the snow fall. It was an impossible thing I needed to do. Impossible, yet I was the only one able to do it. The only one strong enough. I put my cloak hood up and looked out the window.

"Thank you, Keeper," I said once more, and then I warped.

28

As usual during the day, the city was alive with activity, but this time it was different. I had warped a few times and found myself not on a tall building, but on the streets of Thera. As the snow fell, people continued to grow restless.

I couldn't stay here on the streets long. I had to alternate from the streets to the rooftops. Surely by now Rema and her people were looking for me in the city, but the added chaos was making it hard.

News seemed to have traveled fast of the Emperor and Empress' death the night before. This wasn't a reason for people to panic, for they believed the Emperor would return from the dead as he had before. More panic was spread by the idea of the Emperor's family being murdered in their own home.

The previous deaths had always happened outside of the palace walls, or on the battlefield, but certainly not where the family was supposed to be at their safest. Homes were being raided, people were being beaten, and anybody who was even thought to be a threat was being handled accordingly.

Some people of Thera were not against their new ruler. Naturally, the people didn't know that Rema intended to rule permanently; they assumed she was only acting Queen until the Emperor was reborn. But they saw her wave of vengeance and quick rally to action as a sign of strength. Strength that they thought Thera needed, in case another kingdom tried to attack before the Emperor's return.

Besides my friends and Remy, only I knew the truth. I was the only person who knew that the Emperor would not be returning, but I had no idea what Rema's end game was for the discovery of people beyond the water.

I warped, finding myself on a building crouching down and looking around. I wish it was nighttime. It would have been easier to remain invisible under the protection of the night and the rain. My friends didn't have much time, and neither did I.

I warped a few buildings more, and was surprised to find guards positioned on the roofs. They were spread out, and all had their swords already drawn. Rema may have seen this as a smart move, but she had her men spread out. It would be easier for me to handle them one at a time instead of all at once. She also hadn't accounted for me having met with a god, and having been given new power.

The guards seemed to be spread out in a circle. No surprise there. The council building was located directly in the middle of a few surrounding buildings, all of which formed a circle of sorts around it. The guards were positioned so that they could see the council building at all sides.

I warped a few feet over and set my eyes on the first guard. I went to draw my dagger and then stopped myself. "Let's see how this goes," I said under my breath as I moved my eyes from the guard to his sword.

I reached inside myself, just as I had always done, and looked for that new power. I found it as easily as if I had been using it for years. The air around the guard's sword warped, and then the sword vanished.

He looked down and around, but it was too late. In an instant his sword reappeared in my hand. I warped from where I was standing to him in a blink and impaled him in the stomach with his own sword. His body shook as the sword went upward through his stomach and out his upper back. I was afraid for a moment. Not of the guards, but of the feeling I got from killing him.

It felt good. *I* felt good. I felt powerful, stronger than ever, and almost unstoppable. I didn't know if it was the curse kicking in, or if it was just this new power, but I went with it. In less time than it took for me to get dressed, all the guards were dead. The first impaled guard got off easy compared to others.

Others lost limbs, and some lost their heads.

The rooftops of Thera were splattered in crimson now, and for some reason it made me wonder who would have the unfortunate job of having to clean it up.

I positioned myself on the highest building so that I could see the council building.

Luckily, the building wasn't grand in design, so, in theory, it would be easy to find my friends inside. I certainly couldn't go in through the entrance, and I couldn't really see inside the windows. I needed a plan. Then it hit me.

Rema had gotten to know me and Ember over the time we'd spent together planning. She knew how we thought. She knew that it would be crazy for a Warper, a person trained to kill and move unseen, to come strolling through the front door like normal. That would likely be the most unguarded area.

I warped to the front of the building. Everything seemed quiet. As I clasped my hand around the large handle, I looked around one more time and silently prayed to the Keeper that this was the right thing to do. Once I would have thought praying to a god was pointless; now I knew better.

The door opened slowly, and creaked so loudly that it echoed around the entrance. The council building was larger on the inside than expected. Not only was it large, but it was, in fact, grand. Large pillars, thicker than trees, stretched from the shiny floor to the domed ceiling. It seemed like it had been deserted or unused for a while, judging from the thick layer of dust on some of the tables and bookshelves.

The good thing was that this wasn't a prison. There were no dungeons here—simply holding rooms used more for debates than lock-up.

A streak of black rushed by me. It was fast, fast enough to collide with me and knock me down as it moved. I warped quickly to a nearby table, and ignored the voice I heard calling to me from that unknown place.

This center table gave me a focal point and kept me off the floor. Even with my new abilities, I could feel my heart beating faster than normal.

There it was a again. A blur, or something like it, that seemed to be a figure of blackness, moving. It darted back and forth around the room. I drew my dagger, and tried to keep up with it as it moved around the room. I had to wait for it to stop, or I'd never be able to touch it.

Before the blur could stop, I heard a noise behind me of something scraping. Something dragging.

Turning around, I could feel tension rise within me as I saw the female Battle Born walking towards me. The sound of something dragging was her axe. The same, larger-than-ever, double-sided axe that she had had before. Her purple eyes fixed on me as she let out that deathly laugh from an unseen mouth.

Before I could react, the blur began to slow down and found itself circling the female Battle Born. Finally, it stopped moving. What I had thought to be fear earlier couldn't compare to what I was feeling now. Another Battle Born, this time a male one, was standing beside his female counterpart.

Two of them. Two Battle Born stood in my way now. Ember had said the males had enhanced reflexes and were fast, but he had never gone into details on just how fast.

The two sets of glowing purple eyes locked on me, and for a second, they seemed to glow brighter. I had begun to think that the male didn't have a weapon, but just at that very moment, he showed his hands. Both were wrapped in what seemed to be some sort of metal. He flexed his hands and moved his fingers, revealing that the metal on his hands led down to his wrists.

When he flexed his hand into a fist, however, sharp spikes sprang from his hands. For a second, I found myself wishing that he had a simple axe.

They began to move closer to me. They moved as if they knew how powerful they were. You could see it in their body language. Confident, and cold. As they moved, they slowly went from walking side by side to spreading out, positioning themselves on either side of me. I knew it was pointless, because they blocked a person's abilities, but something told me to try anyway.

I reached inside myself, searching for my power and expecting it not to be there—but it was!

Strong and pulsating, like a second heartbeat. Not only was my warping power there, but my new warping abilities, too. Both were still there, seemingly unaffected by the Battle Born. I didn't understand why, and I didn't care.

What I did do was warp the axe from the female Battle Born. It appeared in my hands and almost dropped me to the floor with its weight.

She stepped back and looked at me. I couldn't see her mouth or any normal features at all, but judging on how she was looking at her hands and then to me, I could gather that she hadn't expected that to happen.

The male Battle Born beside me didn't move. He seemed as surprised as her. I wrapped both hands around the axe and began to spin around to gather momentum. As I did so, I warped, appearing in front of the female Battle Born, still spinning. My arms had begun to feel like string, and my shoulder, the one I had been shot in, had begun to hurt again—but the axe found its mark.

The sound the axe made as it sliced through her midsection was hollow and empty. There were no normal sounds of liquid and organs being touched. There was nothing, not even any blood. I tried to pull the axe from her stomach, but I couldn't. It was buried too deep. She fell to her knees and then landed on her side.

She wasn't dead. Her hands still twitched some as she tried to reach for the axe that now called her stomach home. The blur of black was on the move again. I spun around the room, trying to find him, but I couldn't. There was a glimpse of black, and then I could feel a fist hit my chest..

The spikes on the hand stung as they entered my skin, and they seemed to make the wound larger as he drew his hand back. I warped away from him, trying to regain myself, but he was on me in an instant. I couldn't take many hits from those spiked fists. He punched me again, and I was just barely able to get out of the way by leaping to the ground and rolling.

As I rolled, I stretched my hand out and warped the Battle Born's glove away. It would have appeared in my hand, but I had to keep rolling. I couldn't afford to stay still.

As soon as I stood up, I could feel another fist collide with my face.

I wiped my nose and spit some of my own blood from my mouth.

"Die," the Battle Born male said as he threw his body at me like a weapon. He, much like the female, had a hollow dead voice that escaped from behind that mask. It was a stretched-out voice, as if he was having trouble breathing as he said the single word.

As his body collided with mine, I was sent flying into one of the large pillars in the room. My head hit it hard as I slumped down to the ground. As I moved, I could hear the thick sticky sound my head made as I moved it. I let my fingers find the back of my head and winced at the pain. It was tender, and blood was on my fingers now.

The female Battle Born was still on the ground, trying to remove the axe. I didn't know what to do, but the male Battle Born was approaching. Before he could use his speed, I sucked up the pain in my head and warped beside the female on the ground. I stood over her as she paused to look up at me. Her eyes glowed fiercely, as if she was trying to shut my powers off again. She wouldn't be able too, though. The Keeper had made sure of that.

I warped the axe from her stomach and let it appear in my hands as I held them up. Just as I remembered, the axe was extremely heavy, and its own weight did all the work. As it appeared in my hand, gravity allowed it to fall down with speed that my muscles alone couldn't muster. It made a loud thud as the axe passed through her skull and stuck to the ground.

A good half of her head was still attached to her body. From the nose down it was still attached. The upper part of her head just rolled away a few inches. It reminded me of a yolar that had been dropped.

Just like the inside of her body, the Battle Born's head didn't bleed. There wasn't even a brain there. Instead, a thin line of smoke or ash escaped from the Battle Born and faded away in the air. I had seen this smoke-like vapor before, but I couldn't remember where.

He was standing there, just looking at the head of the fallen Battle Born. The eyes were no longer purple on the upper part of the skull. Instead, they were a jet black color. Two lifeless orbs.

He was a blur of speed as he came at me. I was ready for this, and, with impressive speed of my own, I drew my throwing knives and sent them his way. I only threw two, both of which he blocked, but as he did so, I warped them both back to myself from out of the air and threw them again.

After throwing them for a second time, I warped in close to him, dagger drawn, and slashed at his neck. Letting those enhanced reflexes show, he leaned back as my attack missed, and he delivered a kick to my stomach. I stumbled, but didn't fall. I warped again to the side of him and sent a punch with my free hand, but again he dipped low under it, and landed a kick to my back that sent me spinning to the ground.

I couldn't stop moving. He was fast, and staying still would be the death of me. As soon as my body touched the floor I warped again, finding myself near a wall and pulling myself to my feet. I warped to him, slashing and stabbing again with my dagger while sending punches with my free hand. Nothing landed. He was so fast, and seemed to jump, dodge, and flip like some sort of animal.

In a last effort, I did the unthinkable, but I had to slow him down. I dropped my dagger to the ground and looked at those glowing purple eyes.

And then I warped them.

The Battle Born male screamed as the purple orbs vanished from his head and appeared in my hands. He must have felt some sort of pain, because that ghoulish scream was still coming from behind the mask.

I looked at the eyes in my hands as they faded and turned black. They fell to the ground. I warped my dagger to myself and then leapt at the Battle Born. He side-stepped the leap, but he almost fell. I spun around, dagger in hand, and sliced at his throat., but nothing really happened. I had forgotten these creatures didn't have blood or internal organs to worry about.

Running to the Battle Born at full speed, I jumped on him, sending us both crashing to the ground. He reached up to me. He may not have been able to see, but he was still able to grab my neck. My shoulder, as well as the rest of my body, was on fire with pain. My head was spinning, and I could feel what I assumed was blood running down my neck.

As his hand began to tighten around my neck, I slashed my dagger again and again on his, hacking away at his neck until my dagger found the ground. The grip on my neck relaxed as his head became detached. It seemed, as with most things, chopping the head off a Battle Born did the trick.

I stood up, just barely. I had to use one of the pillars for support. I could hardly move, and only hoped that no other guards or Battle Born stood in my way. I didn't have the energy to fight anymore, and I could only ignore so much pain.

I made my way down the adjoining hall of the council building and finally found the holding areas. They were large rooms, with one wall made of glass, allowing the people inside the room and outside the room to see each other. In the center of the glass were several small holes. I guessed it was for air, and for people to be able to talk.

The first two rooms that I came to were empty. The third room, however, wasn't.

The people in the room seemed to jump as I slumped on the outer side of the glass. There was a body on the floor closer to the glass.

I could feel my eyes become blurred with tears, and my breathing seemed short, as I looked at Jolin's lifeless body on the ground.

He was still wearing his suit, and he had the gag in his mouth from earlier. His throat had been slashed and he apparently had been left there to bleed out on himself. I banged my hand on the glass. He didn't deserve this. He didn't deserve to die like an animal.

I looked up from him and saw Vida. She was sitting on a chair. Her face was bruised again, as if she had been fighting, and her eyes were red. She had been crying, but now she wasn't.

She didn't seem scared, and she didn't even flinch as the knife at her throat pushed against her skin. I looked to the person standing behind Vida. The person holding the knife and Vida's life in her hands.

"I knew you'd come. I'm just surprised my fool brother didn't join you," Rema said.

29

"You just couldn't die, could you?" Rema said as she watched me. "This plan took so long to come to light and you, a novice, seem to keep getting in the way. Keeper! Even Ember was easier to get rid of than you." At these last words she pushed the blade of the knife a little harder to Vida's neck.

"You have to know you can't make it out of this situation, Rema. Your guards are dead," I said, but she just smiled.

"No, *those* guards are dead. They rotate on the hour, and the new arrivals should be here any moment."

My instinct was to turn and check the entrance to the holding area, but I didn't. I didn't want her to feel like she had the power here, even if she did.

Rema didn't look like her normal self. She had on that armor again, and she looked like she had been up for days on end. Her breathing was heavy, and blood was staining her hair. I wasn't sure where the blood had come from, but I was willing to bet that it was Jolin's.

"What I don't understand," Rema said, as she leaned and looked up the hall through the glass wall facing me, "is where the Battle Born are, or how you got past them. They are usually—" She stopped speaking as she looked at me.

Me—bruised, bloody, and barely standing up straight, but for the first time she was seeing a smirk on my face. Her eyes seemed to dart from me, as if she realized something that I hadn't yet. A flicker of hope crossed Vida's face as she looked at me and her brow rose.

"They're dead. Both of them," I said calmly.

"Liar!" Rema hissed at me through gritted teeth. She spat when she said it, and the blade pushed deeper into Vida's neck as Rema's other hand clamped down on her shoulder.

"No, I'm not lying. It wasn't easy. I mean, look at me."

I limped closer to the glass and then warped to the other side. It made her flinch a little as I did so. For the first time, Vida was truly smiling now. There was no doubt about it. Then I knew why. Battle Born blocked a person's abilities. But now—

Vida's hand shot up and clasped Rema's. But it wasn't Vida's hand. It was a large, massive, strong hand. Almost twice the size of Vida's. It was bigger than my hand, too.

Rema winced as her hand was crushed under the newfound strength Vida was calling to her aid. I was thankful. I could feel myself slowly moving to a wall and sliding down to the floor. Even that small warp had made me tired.

Vida smiled as she continued to change and use her power. Rema's knife dropped and clattered to the ground and rolled near my feet. I realized this was the dagger that had killed Jolin, and I kicked it away from me with my foot.

Vida had disappeared now. What stood in her place was the massive, hulking body of the guard Bren. Vida continued to squeeze Rema's hand, using her new strength to push her up against the wall. She used her other hand and clasped it around Rema's neck.

Rema tried to talk, but she couldn't get air. Vida released Rema's other hand and allowed both her hands to find her throat now. Vida had begun to turn red as he applied pressure and lifted Rema slightly off the ground.

"This is for Jolin, and Ember." Vida's broken words

echoed around the room in her own feminine voice. Rema slapped her hands at Bren's repeatedly, but had no luck in freeing herself. Her face began to turn colors as her eyes bulged.

Rema's feet were kicking harder now; some of the movements even hit Vida in the leg, but she seemed to not even feel them. Then, they began to slow down. Her hands fell to her side and her feet began to hang. Her entire body was limp now. In a way, she reminded me of a doll being held by a large child.

Bren dropped her body to the floor and then kicked it for good measure. He turned away from Rema and, as he did so, he changed again into a face I had grown so fond of.

Vida ran to me and fell to the ground in front of me. "Warps," she said as she held my face and looked at me.

"I want to kiss you. I just can't find a place on your face that isn't covered in blood."

"If it means anything, only about half of it is mine," I said as I took the hand that she had extended out to me. I flinched and winced as she helped me up from the ground.

I threw my arm around Vida as we looked at Jolin.

"He didn't beg or show any fear," Vida said. "Even when she said his family would never return to its former glory. We can come back and get him," she said. "We have to get out of here before those other guards come."

I agreed with her, even though the sound I made was more of a grunt than words.

We turned to face the door, and Vida screamed as she let me fall to the ground. I tumbled down like a bag full of rocks. She had her fist up ready to attack in an instant.

"Who—" She searched for words. "Where did—who?"

A small boy stepped from the corner of the room. The corner was well lit, and yet we hadn't seen the boy before.

But I knew him.

"Keeper," I said as I pushed myself from the ground.

"What?" Vida said. She stood in front of me as the youth walked towards me. "I'm telling you, kid, back up. I don't like people that sneak up on me, and I will hit a child."

"It's okay Vida," the boy said. "I wish you no harm."

Her fist still raised, Vida tilted her head some.

"We can trust him, Vida. He's a friend."

She stepped aside and allowed the boy to drop down and face me.

"You freed your friends. But we have much work to do still. When you are done here, come meet me at Ember's home. We will talk of what is to come." He placed a hand on my cheek, and I felt warmth. As if I were standing in the sun, basking in its rays. It flooded my body as the pain went away.

"Keeper!" Vida said as she watched my wounds close and the blood on my skin vanish. I don't think she knew just how right she was.

As the Keeper stood to turn away, I reached for him. I didn't touch him, but he did stop. I looked to him and then to Jolin.

"Can you bring him back? Can you?"

He looked at Jolin.

"In a way, of sorts. But it will not be easy or painless. For him or for you."

"For me?" I asked.

He nodded. "His life force is almost gone. While people consider me a god, I didn't create human life. That is a power even greater than mine. What I can do is restore energy and heal, effectively giving him life."

"Then why would it painful for me?" I asked.

"Not just you," he said as he looked to Vida. "You both,

like many people, wield shallow versions of my abilities. You both have a portion of my essence in you. I will take a small portion of this essence from you and give it to him."

"And this is painful?" I asked as I stood and moved to Vida's side.

The Keeper nodded as he looked at us. "The human soul is very much real, and part of my essence is bonded to it. I will have to rip some of it from you to give to him. Though his body is damaged, and he no longer breathes, a person isn't truly gone until their soul leaves. His soul is fading, but is still within him, and if we don't do it now, we won't be able to."

I could feel Vida's fingers locking in mine as she grabbed my hand and looked at me. She had no idea who this person was, but she seemed to believe me, and that was enough for her.

"Do it," she said.

Without even hesitating, he held his hands up and they began to glow—and so did our bodies. We both screamed out. The pain I felt was like nothing that I had ever felt before.

It was as if I was being burned from the inside out. Tears ran down my face, and blood dripped from my nose my ears.

Then it was over. Vida and I were both breathing hard and covered in sweat now. The Keeper held out one glowing hand and walked over to Jolin. He placed the glowing hand on Jolin's stomach and allowed the glow to hover. Jolin's body became transparent for a moment, as if he were made out of glass.

We could see the glowing orb transfer from the Keeper's hand into Jolin's body. The orb seemed to sit in his stomach, as if it were thinking on what to do next, and then it broke into different portions, each portion moving to a different location.

It all began to glow.

The Keeper stood and moved away from Jolin as the orbs continued to pulsate. The glow of the orbs slowly began to go dim, and I saw a slight twitch of Jolin's leg. Vida must have seen this too, because I heard her gasp.

"What?" Jolin said slowly as he came to, putting his hand to his neck. He turned his head in every direction as his eyes opened.

I moved closer to him, followed by Vida. "I leave you alone for a little bit and this is what happens," I said to him as I helped him up.

"Yes, Mr. Lox. My day took a turn for the worse while you were away slaying Emperors," Jolin said. He coughed a little and looked over and saw Rema on the ground.

He exhaled and smiled as he looked at her.

"He's gone," Vida said as she looked around the room. She was right. I hadn't noticed, but the Keeper had left silently once again.

"Who?" Jolin asked.

"We'll explain later," I said. "Come on." I threw his arm over my shoulder. "Let's get you outside, and then I can warp us someplace safe."

"Warp us?" Vida asked.

"Another part of the story I will have to explain later," I said to her as I slowly walked with Jolin.

Vida brought up the rear as we continued to make our way back through the council building. As we moved past the bodies of the Battle Born, Vida and Jolin took long hard looks at their bodies. "There's no blood," Vida exclaimed.

"You certainly have been busy, Mr. Lox." Jolin said. "Busy indeed."

Vida opened the door for us. I was expecting sunshine; I was expecting snow and fresh air.

What I found was Remy, surrounded by guards and some members of the council. I could tell they were council members from the long green robes they wore and their bald tattooed heads. All council members seemed to look the same. Then, to the side, I noticed over a dozen other council members, tied up and sitting on the ground. Beside them were just as many guards, tied up as well.

Remy clapped his hands as he walked to me. "By the Keeper, you did it!" he said as he hugged me and Jolin at the same time.

"You have no idea," I said under my breath.

"What's all this, Remy?" Vida asked.

"This was to be the rescue party, but it seems Lox had everything under control," Remy replied. He looked me in the eye and leaned into my ear. "Is my sister's body in there?"

I nodded.

"Good man," he replied as he patted my shoulder.

"I suppose you will be King now that she is gone," I said as he walked away. He wagged his finger in the air and turned to me.

"Me? King? Keeper, no. I've told you all, power isn't something I seek. No, our new King is resting on your shoulders."

Vida and I both looked to Jolin as he looked up to Remy.

"Jolin is the only other high noble Thera has," Remy continued. "It's his birthright, if he wants it. He will have a lot to learn, but anything is possible."

Jolin slowly removed his arm from my shoulder. He walked forward and was assisted by some of the council members.

"We have some things to discuss, Mr. Remy," Jolin said as he walked by.

"We do, your majesty," Remy said with a smile.

He followed behind Jolin for a few steps, and then came back to me.

"I have reached out to those loyal to me in other kingdoms. We still have no word on Ember. If he is alive, we don't know where he is."

I nodded my head and shook his hand. I had decided in my head that Ember was gone. If he were alive, he would have been here.

I didn't need a body or confirmation. His memory would live on with me, as well as his teachings. I was my own man now. A Warper like no other, and I would have to make my own way.

"So what now, Warps?" Vida said as she walked up and nudged me with her hip.

I looked down at her beside me. Her brown eyes were perfect, and so was her face. I hadn't noticed, but she was healed now, too. It must have happened when the Keeper took our essence.

She looked almost innocent as the snow fell on her cheeks and melted. You'd never know she had just choked the life out of a woman.

"I have to head over to Ember's home and sort some stuff out. After that, I have to find my family and let them know they can return home."

"Need some help with that?" she asked me.

"Are you asking to meet my mother?" I said as I laughed.

She shrugged.

"No," I said, still laughing. "I want you to go with Jolin,

248

if you don't mind. I want to make sure the new king is protected. I trust Remy, but I trusted his sister, too. I want to make sure everything is okay."

"I can do that," she said as she began to change. Her face was reforming into that of an older man.

"Wait," I said, and she stopped and reverted back to herself. She looked up to me once more, and I kissed her, and pulled her close. She was the one thing I had that made sense to me now.

Her life was as crazy and blood-filled as mine, and I was okay with that. As I kissed her in the snow, I wasn't worried about killing, about contracts, about gods, about mysterious civilizations beyond the water. As I kissed her I was simply a man, and I was happy.

EPILOGUE

I reappeared on the roof of Ember's home. For some reason, I was expecting the Keeper to be inside, but he wasn't. As I materialized, I saw him, instead, sitting on the ledge, feet swinging, his head tilted back so that the snow could fall in his mouth. Gods were strange.

"Thanks for coming," he said, without even looking at me. He did continue to move his head back and forth as he tried to catch more snow.

"I can't really tell a god no, now, can I," I asked as I walked closer to him.

"You know, we didn't start out that way. We were just four kids once. Four kids playing in a field when we were supposed to be doing something else." I remembered the four children I had seen. "Then we found something— something that changed us forever."

He leaned over the ledge, looking up the street. I looked, too, but didn't see anything.

"I could go into greater detail, but I will save that for our next meeting. We don't have much time, because you have an old friend coming, any moment now."

"I do?" I asked as my brow rose. He didn't reply.

"He's the reason it always snows and rains, you know. It's something one of the other gods did. His name is Grimsby Glen. He has a thing for snow and rain. Don't ask me why. He is also the one who has been talking to you while you warp."

My head jerked as he said this. "The voice I've been hearing is real?"

The Keeper shook his head. "That opening we found that day, from which something came and changed us into gods—we called it the Rift. It's another plane, another world."

It came to me now. The same smoke-like substance I had seen in the vision. It had looked just like the vapor that had left the fallen Battle Born.

"The Rift is where Warpers go for that instant when they warp. They leave this world, travel through The Rift, and then reappear here."

On the one hand, I wanted to learn more about this Rift; on the other hand, I was scared of the fact that another god had been reaching out to me from some unknown place.

"Grimsby was the strongest of us all, and had a unique bond with the Rift, since he was the first to experience it." I saw the vision again of the youth who had been lifted off the ground. He had looked even younger than the Keeper did.

"I fear it is also he who is controlling the people beyond the waters, and that it was he who was influencing Rema and the Empress Selen Nal. These Battle Born, as you call them, are his weak, lesser creations."

The Keeper stood up from the ledge and removed the excess wetness from his face.

"You have been blessed by me, as people say, and possess some of my essence. More than any person alive," he said as he smiled at me. "Grimsby cannot harm you as easily because of this, nor can he influence you like he wants to. He will try to bring you to his side, and may continue to speak to you when you warp. But you have nothing to fear."

The Keeper looked over his shoulder, back up the

street again. "Right on schedule," he said. "I'll leave you to it, then." He walked past me.

"So that's it? What now?" I said. As I did so, I was reminded of Vida, who had asked me the same thing before I left her.

The Keeper turned to me. "We have much work to do in the future. For now, you must be there for Jolin and for Thera. Changes are coming that even I can't see, but you will have Vida, Remy, and others to help you."

"I'm not a hero," I said. And I wasn't. I was trained to be a killer, born to be a killer. Cursed to be a killer.

"You're right—you're not a hero. I see that now. That's why you are needed. Some things that must be done are not heroic. Now go." He nodded his head to the street again, and then warped away.

I turned and looked to the street again. Finally, I was able to see something. It was a person. This guest the Keeper spoke of. I walked over to the ledge and waited for the person to come into view.

I could barely make out the face, but I knew that hat. I knew the tune he was whistling, and I knew the cane he swung around. The cane that housed a blade on the inside.

It was Ashland. My first true contract. The same man who liked to cut women for fun. He had escaped death.

The Keeper had known he was coming here. Ashland continued to walk, carefree, as he swung his cane. A woman walked by him, and he turned to watch her walk away before he continued. He didn't know that this would be his last day in this world. That this would be his last time seeing snowfall.

I put my hood up and drew my dagger. As he walked, I felt the power brewing inside me. A raging fire ready to be set free, and I let it loose.

I warped.

www.ingramcontent.com/pod-product-compliance
Lightning Source LLC
Chambersburg PA
CBHW020403120726
47904CB00002B/687